FROM NOW UNTIL FOREVER

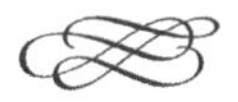

ALEXA RIVERS

From Now Until Forever.

Cover by Shannon Passmore at Shanoff Designs

Editing by Carol Davis and Paper Poppy Editorial.

To Mum and Dad.
For teaching me to believe
that I can do anything.

CHAPTER 1

No. No, no, no.

Sophie Delaware clapped her hands over her eyes and turned away from the window of her boyfriend's office. *This can't be happening. Not now.* Sophie and Evan's relationship was stronger than ever. Or so she'd thought. What she'd just witnessed suggested otherwise. She stood, rooted to the floor, clutching her coat tightly around herself as if it would provide a shield against his betrayal. Bile rose in the back of her throat, and she gagged.

Finally, her feet unstuck from the floor, and she backed away from Evan's office, staggered down the stairs, and yanked on her car door. When it refused to open, she swore and tugged harder. Then she remembered it was locked and fumbled in her coat for the key. Her hands were shaking so badly, it took three attempts to slot the key into the lock. She dropped into the driver's seat and without buckling her seatbelt, slammed her foot on the accelerator and screeched away.

Sophie was driving too fast, but she didn't care. She had to get away from that place, scrub the things she'd seen from her memory and pretend it hadn't happened.

Why does this always happen?

Again and again, over and over, she was constantly waiting for the other shoe to drop.

Sophie shuddered and scrunched her eyes shut, then flinched in fright when the car veered to the left.

"Shit!" She slammed on the brakes, then leaned over the steering wheel to catch her breath. "Damn it!" Fury burned through her veins, and she came upright and punched the steering wheel hard enough that her fist throbbed. "Bloody hell!"

She smacked the steering wheel again and again. Her fist landed on the horn, which blared loudly in the quiet night. Startled, she changed tactics and turned her fists on herself, thumping her thighs and feeling a sick sense of satisfaction at the pain that spiked up her legs. Eventually, she collapsed against the steering wheel, exhausted, and gave in to the crushing sense of defeat.

Why does this happen to me?

Sophie hadn't loved Evan, not as much as she should have, but he'd been her security blanket: a lawyer with a decent income and a respectable business. She'd cared for him. Hoped he cared for her. But Sophie didn't believe in romantic love. Never had. All she wanted was someone to belong to, someone who could take control for a change. She was sick of being the responsible one. For years, she had put others first. She'd never left Itirangi, her small New Zealand home town, because her sick mother needed her. She'd been loyal to her boyfriends, even when they didn't deserve it, and never demanded too much from anyone. Was it too much to ask for someone to treat her the same way?

She could have—and had—forgiven Evan a lot, but she would never be able to erase that image from her mind, and if she couldn't forget, she couldn't forgive. She floundered, with no idea what to do. She couldn't stay here by the side of the road and pretend it had never happened.

Sophie growled in frustration. Her on-again off-again relationship with Evan had taken up most of her energy for three years, and he'd obliterated it all in one fell swoop.

What would life look like without him?

Sophie had no idea.

What she did know was that she couldn't sit in her car all night and going home seemed like a bleak prospect. She could drive around aimlessly, but the temptation to drive out of town and keep on going might get the better of her, and she couldn't leave her mother, Antonia, behind to fend for herself. While she might resent her mother sometimes, she loved her, too.

Turning to her friend, Avery, wasn't an option. The 'I told you so' talk was never fun.

That left Aria, her childhood friend, always ready with a kind word and a supportive hug. Aria's fiancée, Eli, and his younger sister, Teri, were out of town, visiting their grandparents, so Aria was alone.

Mind made up, Sophie steadied her breathing and eased her foot off the brake, setting out with new purpose. Aria would be there for her. They could snuggle up on the couch with ice cream and watch Sandra Bullock movies. It would be therapeutic.

Sophie paid extra attention to the road. She didn't want any more almost-accidents. Hands trembling on the steering wheel, she cruised across town at forty kilometers an hour until she reached Aria's driveway and rolled to a halt. The house was dark, but Aria would get out of bed for her, no question about it.

Sophie took the bottle of wine intended for her date with Evan and knocked on the door. No answer, and it was locked. The house was empty. Sighing, Sophie sank onto the ratty sofa on the front porch and tucked her feet beneath her. Wherever she was, Aria would be home soon.

She withdrew the bottle of wine tucked beneath her arm

and twisted the lid off to take a fortifying gulp. The wine slid down her throat easily and was surprisingly refreshing. Swigging down another mouthful, Sophie mentally reviewed her dating history. She'd had a few lovers, but only three serious relationships. One had ended when her boyfriend tried to date Sophie *and* her friend at the same time. The second, a long-distance relationship with a university academic, had ended when his unrealistic expectations exhausted her. Relationship number three was with that cheating, lying pig, Evan.

Sophie wondered how she'd ended up with such a dismal dating record. Cheated on more often than not. How depressing.

Taking another sip of wine, she hoped Aria would be back before long. Goosebumps had broken out on her exposed legs, and although she was in a masochistic mood, she wasn't prepared to freeze her ass off. Maybe she should just go home.

Wait.

She heard footsteps. Loud footsteps. They didn't belong to Aria; Sophie would recognize the sound of her friend's footsteps anywhere. These were heavier, stronger, more... male. They were coming from behind the house.

There weren't many reasons for a man to be lurking outside a woman's house in the dark, and even though Sophie was partially hidden on the sofa, the footsteps scared her. She screwed the lid back on the wine and tiptoed around to stand behind the porch, in the darkest shadows, wielding the bottle like a weapon.

The footsteps grew louder but also slower, like the man knew she was there and was waiting to see what would happen. Sophie edged forward, careful to stay in the shadows, then stretched her neck and peered around the corner. Against the dim streetlight, she could make out the silhouette of a very large man. His shoulders were broad, and he stood well over six-feet-tall. Probably six-three or six-four. More than a foot taller than she was. In a confrontation, she stood no chance of winning. Better to take him by surprise.

Without thinking about it long enough to change her mind, Sophie held the bottle like a baseball bat and jumped out from her hiding spot, screaming at the top of her lungs.

~

COOPER SIMONS DIDN'T HAVE the foggiest idea what to do when he was confronted by a harpy wielding a half-empty bottle of wine and screaming. Should he be scared? Horrified? Amused? Somehow, he doubted 'amused' was the correct response.

"I'm not here to hurt you," he said gently. Pacifying the harpy was at the top of his to-do list. "You can put the bottle down. I'm not going to hurt you."

"Then why are you hiding in the bushes?" The harpy's voice shook, but he sensed that she was second-guessing the need to bonk him over the head and gut him.

"I wasn't hiding in the bushes," he replied, taking a step closer to get a better look at her. Other than her wide eyes and shallow breathing, she seemed normal. Wait...was that...

"Sophie?" he asked.

"Yeah?" She lowered the bottle until it hung by her side, her left hand clasping her trench coat closed so tightly, her knuckles went white.

"It's Coop," he told her. "Cooper Simons."

"Oh." Sophie grimaced and shook her head in self-disgust. "Now I feel like an idiot."

"Are you okay?" Despite recognizing the crazy woman as one of his sister's closest friends, he remembered how disturbed she'd looked a moment earlier.

"I'm having a really shitty day," she admitted. "I came to visit Aria, but she's not here, so I was waiting on the porch..."

She trailed off, then shrugged. "I may have overreacted. Sorry."

Cooper edged forward and held out a hand, palm facing upward, non-threatening. "Bottle, please."

It took a few moments for his meaning to sink in, then Sophie slapped the bottle into his palm. "I'm so sorry," she said sheepishly.

He set the bottle on the ground, then inched closer, taking care not to startle her. Her eyes tracked him, but she didn't back away. Sophie's bare legs beneath her coat—which only reached mid-thigh—made her look small and vulnerable. And cold. The temperature had dropped rapidly since sundown, and there would be a frost by morning. She must be *frozen*.

Cooper slung an arm around Sophie's shoulders and led her back up onto the porch. He pushed her softly down onto the sofa, and she tucked her feet beneath her butt. Cooper shucked his jacket and laid it over her exposed legs.

"Oh, you don't need to do that!" she exclaimed. "I'm fine. I don't want you freezing on my behalf."

"I insist," Cooper replied, smiling when she stared at him in disbelief. "I'm a gentleman. I couldn't live with myself if I let a woman be cold while I'm toasty warm."

He expected her to be pleased by the sentiment, so he was shocked when she scowled and rolled her eyes. "Yeah, right," she said. "Gentlemen don't exist. You're all the same: a bunch of misogynistic pricks who think with their dicks."

Cooper smothered a laugh, compelled to defend his gender. "We're not so bad. Most of us are nice once you get to know us. It's not our fault we get distracted by pretty faces."

"Pretty faces," Sophie spat, her expression outraged. "Like I'd believe that! Boobs and butts, that's all men care about. Long legs, great. Cold heart? Who gives a shit, right?"

"Men appreciate beautiful women," Cooper agreed,

feeling strangely like she was leading him into a trap. "Maybe we let them get away with stuff because we like to look at them. Where's the harm in that?"

"What about the rest of us?" Sophie demanded. "Do we deserve to be treated badly because we aren't a perfect ten?"

"Of course not."

Was he supposed to be agreeing, or playing devil's advocate? Cooper had no idea. Clearly, something had pissed Sophie off. Presumably a man, given her animosity towards him. Though now that he'd thought that, with the way his luck had gone today, he could well have said something offensive and not known it. Damn confusing creatures, women.

Cooper had sought out Aria for much the same reason as Sophie: comfort and reassurance. He'd broken things off with Gemma, a sexy nurse who worked at the hospital, and damn, had she taken it badly. Spouting nonsense about how he used women for his own benefit, how he'd end up old and alone. For Christ's sake, he *loved* women. Which was part of the problem, of course. Unfortunately, he didn't always know the best approach when dealing with their emotions.

He opted for a sympathetic approach. "What happened, Sophie?"

"Nothing happened," she snapped.

"Come on," he prompted. "Clearly, you're upset. Want to talk about it?"

"No."

She said nothing else. The silence stretched for over a minute and started to become awkward. Cooper was wondering what tactic to try next when she spoke again.

"Men are sleazeballs."

Leaning back against the couch, Cooper regarded her thoughtfully, and Sophie pointedly looked the other way. It had been years since he'd had anything much to do with her. Back in high school, she'd been a fixture in his life, as all

Aria's friends had been. The Simons' home had been a popular hangout because his mother, Donna, kept the pantry stocked with home-baked goodies, and his father, Geoff, was keen to put on barbeques or umpire sports games.

After high school, Cooper had joined the army, and spent three years training and six years in active service. He'd been to Iran, Iraq, Syria, and Afghanistan, places he'd gladly forget if he could. At twenty-seven, he'd returned home having seen more death and destruction than most people did in a lifetime. It was enough to make a man sick. Two years on, he still remembered the dust and despair.

In the years he'd been back, he hadn't seen much of Sophie. He remembered Aria saying something about a controlling boyfriend, and Cooper wracked his brain, trying to remember. Hell, he hadn't even noticed she hadn't been around much. All things considered, Sophie was virtually a stranger to him. How was he supposed to handle this?

SOPHIE SNUGGLED beneath Cooper's jacket, which was still warm from his body. The man himself was as silent as a rock. He sat at the far end of the couch, putting as much distance between them as possible, and seemed to be waiting for her to regain her sanity. Either that or lose it completely and begin dancing around naked and chanting prayers in some mysterious language. The heavy silence was unendurable, and although she knew she had put him in a difficult position, she was angry with him for not saying something. *Anything.*

"You've got that strong, silent thing down to an art," she said finally.

"No one would believe you if you told them that," he replied. "I'm the family gossip, after all."

"Yeah, right," she muttered. "You're the family playboy."

"Is that what the ladies are saying?"

He sounded amused by the prospect, and Sophie turned her head until she was facing him again. Most of the tears that had gathered in her eyes were gone, but she was pretty sure a snot bubble was hanging from her nose.

"As if you don't know that." Her voice had a hard edge, even though she'd meant to tease him. "You've got that buff, sexy thing going on. Add in your charming personality, and I'm surprised women's pants don't magically fall down when you pass them in the street."

"You think they don't?"

His eyes twinkled mischievously, and Sophie almost smiled. "That's exactly what I mean. All you men think about is sex."

"What's going on, Soph?" The nickname slid off his tongue easily, and she liked the way it sounded. Not many men dared to shorten her name.

"Man troubles," she explained. "I'll get over it."

"Vent to me," he offered. "I don't mind being used as a verbal punching bag."

"That's nice of you, but you don't have to listen to my problems."

"Wait a moment." Cooper left the couch, strode out of view and returned with the bottle of wine. "More comfortable now?" he asked, handing it to her.

"Are you kidding? I've got booze and a hot man. What else do I need?"

She was deflecting, and she was sure he knew it.

"Tell me what's wrong."

This time it wasn't a request, but a command. Surprising herself, Sophie obeyed. "Evan cheated on me."

"I'm sorry."

Searching his eyes, she saw genuine sympathy. "It's not like things have been great between us," she said. "But I can't believe he'd cheat on me. I'm so stupid." Choking on a rising wave of emotion, she fought to continue. "Since we got back together, we've been taking it slow. No sex. It was my idea. Tonight, I decided we'd waited long enough, so I went to surprise him at his office." She shrugged helplessly. "He was with his secretary. You know, *with*. And now that picture is burned into my brain. Couldn't he just wait a couple of weeks for me? Was that too much to ask? You're a guy. What do you think?"

"Great way to put me on the spot," Cooper said good-naturedly. "I don't want to be responsible for a woman hating men for the rest of her life."

"Seriously, Coop."

"Seriously, Soph," he mimicked her. "I don't do long-term relationships. I haven't got a clue. I think he should have broken up with you if he wanted to be with someone else, but that's as far as I'll go."

~

COOPER WATCHED Sophie digest his words. Clearly, she needed some insight into the male mind.

"Have you ever cheated?" she asked.

"I copied Michael Portman's answers on the senior calculus exam."

"You know what I mean," she said irritably. "Have you cheated on a girl?"

"I had sex with my girlfriend and her best friend at the same time once. Does that count?"

Sophie shook her head as if he were a lost cause. "You're disgusting."

"I'm a connoisseur of women." Except that after that awful episode with Gemma, he was beginning to wonder: What if all the women he dated ended up hating him? Most of them took the breakup well because they'd known it was coming. Cooper never hid his intentions. Women knew the arrangement was only temporary, but maybe they hoped for more.

"Whatever you say."

She obviously thought he was full of shit, that he was leaving a trail of broken hearts behind him. Hardly fair, but he couldn't blame her, given what she'd been through.

"I'm sorry you have to be here for this," she said abruptly. "It must not be much fun for you."

"I can think of worse things to do with my time."

"Really?" She raised an eyebrow, as if she were daring him to come up with something worse than listening to his sister's friend complain about men.

"I could be forced to watch *Downton Abbey* reruns while drinking margaritas and painting my toenails."

Sophie laughed, her sense of humor returning. "I really am sorry."

"Forget about it," he told her. "Now, how about you get in my car and I drive you home?"

She nodded. *Thank God*, he thought. She wasn't in a good state to drive, and he'd never be able to show his face at his parents' place again if he didn't see her home safely.

"Thanks." Standing, she gave him back his jacket, then followed him to the car. "You're not such a bad guy, Cooper Simons."

He winked, the thought buoying him. "Let's make that our little secret."

CHAPTER 2

Sophie woke to find herself hanging off the side of the bed. One arm and leg were slung across the top of the mattress, while the others dangled off the edge, and her hand was brushing the floor. The blankets were tangled in a heap around her.

The phone rang shrilly, cutting through the quiet. With an 'oomph', Sophie slipped off the bed and landed on the floor, taking with her the blankets, which slid beneath her feet as she stumbled across the room and grabbed the phone.

"Hello," she answered sleepily.

"Sophie?" It was a woman's voice. The upwards inflection indicated she was concerned.

"Whosit?" she mumbled, wiping her eyes and peering blearily at the screen. "Whatimesit?"

"It's Aria." Now, she sounded amused. "And it's ten o'clock. Most of us have been up for a couple of hours."

"You wouldn't have been up for a couple of hours if Eli were there," Sophie retorted, slowly awakening. At least, *she* sure wouldn't have been. Eli was *hot*, and despite Aria's good-girl-next-door persona, Sophie suspected she and Eli were animals in the sack.

Aria sighed. "If Eli were here, I wouldn't be on the phone with you."

Laughing, Sophie carried the phone back to bed, wrapped her polar fleece bathrobe around herself and sat cross-legged on the mattress. "Sisters before Misters," she said.

"You obviously haven't been with *my* Mister," Aria replied. "If you had, you wouldn't be saying that."

"Don't rub it in." Sophie groaned. "And don't take that the wrong way. I don't have a thing for Eli. But I wish I had someone that yummy in my bed."

"What about Evan? He's no Eli, but he's not bad."

"Ugh." Flashbacks. The betrayal, the horror. Sophie shuddered, feeling like there were insects crawling over her skin. Disgusting, slimy little insects. Just like Evan. "Let's not even go there."

"What is it, honey? Cooper called and said you were here last night. He was worried about you."

Big-mouthed good-for-nothing men. None of them could be trusted. "Evan cheated on me," she admitted, drawing the robe more tightly closed. "I walked in on it. Well, kind of. He didn't know I was there, but I got an eyeful of him and his secretary."

"I'm so sorry." Aria's tone was sympathetic, but also unsurprised. None of Sophie's friends had liked Evan. Avery was open about it, but Aria hadn't approved, either; she'd just been better at hiding it. "How are you holding up?"

Sophie frowned at herself in the mirror across the room. Flat hair, a shade off ginger, was plastered to her face. Her eyes were red and puffy. "Crappy," she said honestly. "I'm such an idiot."

"No, you're not." The statement could have been more convincing, Sophie thought. "You see the best in people."

Sophie harrumphed. "Not people in general. Just slimeball men who want to pull the wool over my eyes."

"Maybe a little. Do you want me to come over? We can watch girl-power movies and eat ice cream."

Aria was suggesting exactly what Sophie had wanted last night. "Thanks, but no," she said. "I think I'll go for a run and do some weights. You know, work out the anger."

"Whatever works for you," Aria replied, her voice full of doubt.

Aria wasn't the biggest fan of exercise. She'd certainly do it when she had to, but she didn't often volunteer to participate. Sophie, on the other hand, found exercising more effective than therapy. By the time she'd run eight kilometers, bench-pressed forty kilos and done a hundred press-ups, she was always too exhausted to be angry or emotional.

"I'll talk to you later," Sophie said.

"Bye, sweetie."

Sophie dragged herself from the bed and dressed in a pair of grey sweatpants and a baggy t-shirt. She fed Cletus, the fat tabby cat she'd rescued from Avery (who'd received him from an ex-boyfriend who hadn't realized that she hated pets, and subsequently, hadn't lasted long). Avery had named the cat Cletus as a public statement of her dislike. Sophie had always intended to change his name, but by the time he came to live with her, he already answered to Cletus. It was unfortunate, but nothing could be done. Come to think of it, Cletus had mauled Evan at every opportunity. The cat was smarter than she was.

Sophie prepared a bowl of cereal and carried it out to her mother in the Big House. The path between the Big House and Sophie's cottage stretched over a wide lawn which was dotted with fruit trees and fringed by a flower garden. During the summer a few years back, their fruit trees had flourished, and in one of her rare moments of domesticity, Antonia had taught Sophie to make apricot jam. They'd made enough to last for years. Now, though, it was autumn, and the leaves had turned gold. The sweet scent of spoiled fruit lingered in the air from apricots that had dropped before Sophie could get around to picking them.

Sophie had grown up in the Big House with Antonia and her policeman father, Mike, a man who'd been soft-spoken and constant. He'd liked to garden, and Sophie had been raised on the home-grown vegetables which she'd helped to gather in the evenings. After her father died, she'd converted the vegetable garden into a lawn, but the patch of grass was a different shade of green from the rest of the lawn. Visitors didn't notice it, but Sophie always did.

Mike had died on the job when Sophie was twelve, leaving her and Antonia alone. Antonia had shut down after the funeral, often staying in bed for days at a time and refusing to see friends or family. Sophie had thought it was a phase, that the grief would eventually fade, and perhaps it would have, except that less than a year after Mike's death, Antonia had been diagnosed with multiple sclerosis and had begun a vicious downward spiral. Fourteen years later, cycling between neuromuscular degeneration and clinical depression, she still couldn't function.

Sophie had moved into the cottage when she turned eighteen to get some distance from her mother. It was selfish, but she couldn't bear to share the Big House. Too many memories, not all of them pleasant. She liked to be nearby, though.

She shouldered the front door open, then crossed the hall to the master bedroom. Antonia lay in the same place as usual, propped up by a stack of pillows, a small figure almost lost in the massive bed. She didn't move. Only her eyes followed Sophie while she set up a table and swung it over the bed, then drew up a chair to join her mother.

"How are you, Mum?" Sophie asked as she uncovered the cereal and placed a cup of tea within Antonia's reach.

Some days, Antonia could feed herself, but on others, she needed to be fed—either because of muscle weakness or lack of willpower—and judging by her lack of response today, she needed help, which meant that Sophie wouldn't get any conversation from her. The humiliation of being hand-fed weighed heavily on her proud mum.

Sophie scooped cereal and lifted it towards her mother's mouth, grateful when she opened and chewed. They continued the feeding process until the meal was gone, and then Sophie helped Antonia drink, assisting her with the glass when her hands trembled.

Before she left, Sophie opened the curtains, helped Antonia shift into a chair, and started Whitney Houston playing on the stereo. Antonia had a beautiful singing voice and loved the divas. Sophie always held out hope that one day she could be coaxed into singing again, and it might bring enough joy to her life to make it feel worthwhile.

WITH HER MORNING ROUTINE FINISHED, Sophie drove to visit Avery. She had no intention of exercising, as she'd told Aria. The truth was, Aria was a sweetheart, and right now Sophie needed some tough love.

On most weekends, Avery could be found in one of two places: her garden, or the laboratory where she worked. The woman didn't know how to relax. She didn't have a social life with the exception of weekly visits to the pub with Aria and Sophie, and occasional weekend get-togethers. During those times, Avery could pretend to be a normal human being rather than a robot.

Sophie loved Avery. Of course she did. But sometimes it seemed as though her friend was made of stone.

Sophie wandered onto the back yard and found Avery weeding her veggie patch. "Nice cabbages," she said, coming to a stop.

"They're too small," Avery replied. "But they'll be worth eating eventually." Her ponytail swished against her back as she turned around. "What brings you here?"

"What?" Sophie raised an eyebrow. "I'm not allowed to visit my friend?"

"Not without an ulterior motive." Avery combed her fingers through her long brown hair and swiped a hand across her forehead, leaving a dirty smudge behind. "So, what is it?"

"Evan cheated on me." Sophie got straight to the point. Avery was blunt and appreciated the same in return.

"Are you surprised?"

"Yes." Sophie sighed and closed her eyes. "No. I don't know. What should I do?" She hated the needy, weak sound of her voice. "I'm so over getting hurt."

"Break up with him," Avery instructed.

"It's not that simple." Even the thought of it was enough to give her heart palpations. "I don't know how to be single."

"You won't be single for long," Avery said. "Only until you get back together with him again."

Sophie flinched away from her. "That's mean. Even for you."

"I'm sorry." And to Avery's credit, she sounded like she meant it. "Look," she continued patiently, "you *need* to break up with him. It's bad for your health to be so stressed."

Sophie grumbled, "And here I thought you were a doctor of philosophy, not a medical doctor."

"I am." Avery smiled and, in an uncharacteristically affectionate move, wrapped her arms around Sophie. "But a bit of common sense is all it takes to see that your relationship is unhealthy."

"I seem to be short in the common-sense department." Sophie teared up again but sniffed and blinked away the tears.

"Luckily for you, I have enough for both of us." Avery released her and walked over to wash her hands under the hose attached to the side of the house. "This is what we're going to do. We're going to dress to kill. I'm going to drive you to Evan's house and wait outside while you break the news to him. If you come back without breaking it off, I'm leaving you there, and you can walk home."

Evan's house was at least a ten-minute drive out of town. A painful walk in the heels Sophie favored.

"Once you've done the deed, we're going to Davy's to drink ten beers each. We're going to play darts really badly and flirt with men we'd never sleep with. Then I'll take you home and crash on the floor outside your bedroom in case you decide to do something stupid like go to Evan and beg him to take you back."

Sophie nodded slowly, liking the sound of this plan—apart from the bit where she might get left in the country to walk home in three-inch heels. She'd just have to make sure that didn't happen.

"What about Mum?" she asked. "She needs lunch and dinner."

Avery shrugged nonchalantly. "Aria will cook her something. You know how she loves to feed people."

"Okay, I'm in."

SOPHIE WAS WEARING a blue summer dress that hugged her waist and flared out around her hips. She let Avery do her makeup, then added more blush and a brighter shade of lipstick. While Avery preferred neutral tones and nude colors, Sophie liked a bit of pizzazz. More than that, she needed it. Otherwise, she'd never attract a man's attention, not when she looked like a cross between a teenager and the girl next door. *The teenager next door.* Just great.

"You can do this," Avery said firmly as they stopped outside Evan's country house, a gorgeous white stone cottage with a chocolate-brown roof and a well-kept garden where roses and daffodils thrived. Twin glass doors on the master bedroom opened onto a wooden deck with a barbecue and a spa pool. Evan didn't deserve such a nice house, but smarmy lawyers often got more than they deserved.

Striding to the door, Sophie held her head high. She'd worn her sexiest stilettos, knowing that the added height would boost her confidence.

"Good morning, Sophie," Evan said with a smile when he opened the door. "You're just in time for lunch. Come in."

"I'd rather not," Sophie replied quietly.

"Excuse me?" Evan leaned closer, as if he hadn't heard her.

He was a handsome devil. Even though he'd screwed her over, she couldn't deny the obvious. With close-cropped hair, a lean frame, brown eyes and the whitest teeth she had ever seen, he cut a nice figure. But Sophie knew he had his teeth professionally whitened twice a year, got a manicure once a month, and waxed his back every other week. His polished looks took effort to maintain. She'd bet his pretty secretary didn't know that.

"I don't want to come in," she said more assertively.

"So, you want to go into town?" he asked, his eyes betraying his confusion.

"I don't want to go anywhere with you."

He frowned. "Then, what are you doing here?"

Sophie swallowed her nerves and met his eyes without wavering. "It's over, Evan. Me and you, we're over. We're not getting back together ever. We're done."

Evan shifted his position to rest his forearm on the door frame so that he towered over her. A move intended to intimidate her, no doubt. "If something has upset you, we can talk about it."

He said that as if it were the most rational thing in the world, and it made Sophie furious.

"There is nothing to talk about," she snapped. "You've made me feel like shit over and over, but I forgave you. Not this time. I won't forgive cheating. I'm finally going to get rid of you from my life. If you ever come to my house, I won't open the door. If you call, I won't answer. Don't bother even thinking about me ever again. Got it?"

"Surely we can work this out." His smile was arrogant. So certain of what she'd do. "You'll miss me, Sophie. You always do."

"It's not going to happen," she warned him. "No matter how much I miss you, I'm not coming back. You can go screw yourself."

Proud of herself for not stuttering or giving him any mixed messages, Sophie almost ran back to the car, teetering on her heels.

"See you soon," Evan called after her.

"Go to hell!" she screamed in return.

The car was still running, and Avery gunned it as soon as Sophie had climbed into the passenger seat.

"Go, Soph!" Avery exclaimed. "You were awesome. I didn't know you had it in you."

"Neither did I," Sophie gasped, short of breath from the adrenaline rush. "I feel great. Now, where's the beer?"

~

"I'M NOT DATING ANYMORE," Cooper announced.

His proclamation was met with laughter from his family.

"I'm serious," he protested. "I'm taking a break from women."

"Cooper," his mother, Donna, said affectionately. "You're my son, and you know I love you, but you can't go more than a few days without female company."

"Of course I can. I'm a man with many interests."

"Most of which involve women," his brother, Justin, muttered.

"I can enjoy myself without a woman," Cooper asserted,

unable to believe that his family thought him incapable of spending a few weeks alone.

"We believe you," Aria, said, but he could tell she wasn't convinced.

"I don't," Teri, Eli's precocious sister, said, tongue-in-cheek.

"I'll make a female friend," he said, changing tack. "That way, I can spend time with a woman without dating."

Justin rolled his eyes. "When was the last time you had a platonic relationship with a woman you weren't related to?"

"When he was nine," his father, Geoff, replied, shuffling a deck of cards.

Cooper looked from his parents to his siblings and back again. None of them had faith in him, but he was going to prove them wrong. After all, he'd managed just fine with Sophie the other night.

"Sophie," he said. "I had a conversation with her and kept her company for at least an hour without trying to get into her pants."

Donna chuckled. "Dear Sophie. She's practically family."

"But she's not," he said pointedly. "And, you know what? If I can be friends with her, I can be friends with other women. Have a little faith."

Saying he was friends with Sophie Delaware might be pushing it, but he'd take all he could get. Perhaps he'd pursue a friendship with her just to prove his case.

His mother was hiding a smile. Aria and Eli, her smitten fiancée, were holding hands in the corner.

Justin smirked and said, "I'll believe it when I see it."

EVERY MORNING WITHOUT FAIL, Cooper woke at 6 a.m. and did a rigorous workout that consisted of weight training and cross-fit techniques. Following that, he went for a five-kilometer run that finished at the café, where he got a smoothie or some green juice to start the day on a high note. The routine worked well for him, and he completed it regardless of how he'd spent the night before.

Halfway through his run alongside the golf course, he spied another runner a hundred meters or so in front of him. From the ponytail and short steps, he could tell it was a woman.

Cooper increased his pace to get a better look at her. Surely, he could appreciate the female form, even if he was taking a break from dating. As he got closer, he decided she must be a regular runner. Her feet fell in an even rhythm, and she didn't slow or stumble over rocks and roots on the dirt track. She might be short, but her legs were long in proportion to her body. They were lightly bronzed and toned, with no extra bits of flesh wobbling as she ran. Tight exercise shorts emphasized her firm but mouth-wateringly-rounded butt. This woman obviously squatted a lot.

Her back was bare and in the same condition as her legs —slim, but with muscles bunching and working beneath the surface. As he drew nearer, he could see beads of sweat on the exposed skin. One droplet trailed from her sweat-drenched tank top down her back and disappeared into the waistband of her shorts.

Cooper swallowed and tore his eyes away. Appreciating a woman's natural beauty was something he did automatically, but it usually didn't turn him on so much. It must be because he knew he couldn't sleep with this woman. At least, not yet. Maybe in a few weeks. With that in mind, Cooper stretched his legs, and easily caught up with her.

"You have excellent form." He spoke without panting, a task he could only accomplish because of his high level of fitness. She glanced towards him, and the curve of her face looked oddly familiar.

~

On Sunday morning, Sophie woke with more dignity, feeling fresh despite the six beers she'd ended up having. She changed into a pair of shorts and a midriff-baring tank top and tiptoed past Avery, who was curled up on a mattress next to the bed. After locking the door behind her, she turned on her iPod and selected her running playlist, which kept her feet moving quickly instead of dragging. The circuit she usually ran began at the police station, circled the golf course, cut through the park and wove along the stream.

Getting outdoors in the morning cleared Sophie's head and prepared her for a hard day of sales. Her job as a real estate agent was increasingly busy, what with the tourist market in Itirangi having picked up lately. The increase in holiday homes and motels in the area hadn't gone down well with all of the locals, but it was good for Sophie, and she remained optimistic that Eli Lockwood's new mall development would speed up the rate of progress in the town.

Sophie had toyed with the idea of turning the Big House into a bed & breakfast to improve her bank balance even further—maybe allowing her to save enough for an overseas holiday or a road trip around New Zealand—but she couldn't. It wouldn't be fair to Antonia to invite strangers into her home.

Sophie ran faster, trying to escape her worries and the anxiety that always crept up on her at the thought of being stuck in this town forever, unable to leave. Itirangi might be home, but Sophie had *never* left. She'd watched her friends go to university, backpack around Europe, or fly over to soak up the sun in Australia, but she'd stayed behind to look after her mother and earn her certificate in real estate over the internet.

Sophie's feet ate up the pavement and sweat dripped from her hair, down the back of her neck. Whenever she ran the circuit, she timed it, and although her times were consistent, she'd seen slow improvement over the past few months.

Heavy metal music screamed through her headphones and she gritted her teeth, pushing a bit harder.

She squealed when someone suddenly appeared at her right. He was too close, and she jerked her headphones off with one hand to confront him. Fright had her heart thumping harder in her chest than it had from exertion.

"I said, you have excellent form."

It was Cooper Simons, sneaking up on her.

Damn, he looked good in workout clothes. The other night, she hadn't paid much attention to anything beyond their conversation. He'd always been a dangerously good-looking guy, but now he was breathtaking, with his blond hair tied back, strands of it hanging around his face, dampened with sweat. She knew it had been cut short when he was in the military, but since he'd returned, he'd grown it long, and now it reached his shoulders.

His almond-shaped blue eyes were focused intently on her, and stubble shaded his strong jaw. The navy-blue shirt he was wearing had tight sleeves which displayed arms corded with muscle. Sophie's gaze followed his body down to equally well-muscled thighs. Her mouth went dry.

"Hey," she said breathily.

"Hey, Sophie."

Was it her imagination, or did he look disappointed? She smiled at him. "I didn't know you ran."

"Every day," he replied, his breathing even. The man was incredibly fit. And incredibly sexy.

Forget it, she told herself. *He's your best friend's brother.*

"I run most days," she told him.

"I can tell." For a moment, his eyes flared with heat, but it was gone so quickly that she decided she'd imagined it.

"Where do you run?" she asked, adjusting her step so she could talk comfortably.

He accommodated her change of pace by switching down

his own. "The golf course circuit, through the park and across to the café."

Sophie grinned, wondering if he fell prey to the mindset so many people did, that exercise justified eating some cake. Somehow, she doubted it. No one who thought that way would have such an impressive body.

"I finish up with a smoothie," he continued. "Have you tried the smoothies from the Berry Barn?"

Sophie shook her head.

"You should."

"Maybe I will."

They ran side by side in silence. Usually, running with a partner annoyed Sophie because they could never keep up with her, but Cooper matched her stride for stride. She snuck another look at him, running her gaze appreciatively up and down his torso. What a beautiful specimen of a man. Sophie had indulged in affairs with men of different shapes and sizes, but none as perfect as he was.

While she wouldn't consider herself an expert in men's bodies, she hadn't been shy about studying every inch of the ones she'd seen up close. What would it be like to be with someone as strong as Cooper? All of a sudden, she wanted to know.

Cooper Simons was notorious for having a different woman on his arm every month. None of them stayed around long enough for his family to bother learning their names. He wasn't the type of guy you had a relationship with, but an affair was a different story.

Sophie considered the idea. All of his lady friends looked blissfully happy until the day he dumped them. He wasn't cruel, and he didn't mean to hurt anyone; it just happened. But if she went into an affair knowing the score, and with an end date in mind, there could be no hurt feelings.

Sophie shook her head, amused by the direction her thoughts were taking. Fantasizing about having a casual affair with her friend's brother was proof she was sex-deprived.

"You're in fantastic shape," she said as they neared the spot where their routes diverged.

He grinned. "I'll take that as a huge compliment, coming from you."

Her stomach flip-flopped. "Coming from me?"

"Don't fish for compliments," he teased. "You must know you're in great shape yourself."

Sophie ducked her head to hide the blush creeping up her cheeks. Curse being a pale-faced ginger. Her face lit up like Rudolph's nose at the slightest bit of provocation.

"Come with me to the café," he said. "Try a smoothie. You'll love them."

"How do you know?" she asked, arching an eyebrow.

"Because I love them," he replied without hesitating. "And I'm starting to think we might have a lot in common."

She rolled her eyes. "You got that from a ten-minute run?"

"I've known you for more than ten years."

"And we've spoken all of half a dozen times." Really, they were nothing more than acquaintances.

"I think we bonded the other night, once you decided I wasn't a serial killer."

Sophie laughed. "I'm sorry about that. I'd say I'm not usually that crazy, but, well..."

"You are," he filled in.

"Exactly." She laughed again. "You'd better be telling the truth about these smoothies."

"I am," he said solemnly. "They're nectar of the gods, I swear."

"Then take me to the smoothies."

They ran next to each other in companionable silence until the path narrowed, then she dropped back a few steps so they were moving single file. From behind, she had a wonderful view of his butt and thighs, which bunched and sprang with each step. She could watch him run forever. Sadly, the path widened again, and she had to give up her view to resume her position beside him.

"The café is a kilometer from the bus stop up ahead," Cooper said. "How about a race? I'll give you a head start."

Sophie gasped, infuriated by the implication that she couldn't keep up with him. "I don't need a head start!"

"Easy now, Shorty," he said, trying to placate her. "Each one of my steps is two of yours."

"Then it's a good thing I can run more than twice as fast as you." The competitive streak she'd always had began to show. They were almost at the bus stop.

"Loser buys the smoothies," Cooper suggested.

Sophie grinned. "You're on. Prepare to lose."

Three more steps, and they came even with the bus stop. Sophie lengthened her stride and drove her legs faster, but not too fast. One kilometer was a reasonable distance, and she didn't want to wear herself out early.

For the next three minutes, they didn't speak; the only noise between them was heavy breathing. Sophie was incredibly aware of the man next to her, of the sweat dripping down his forehead and the quick breaths he took. She imagined he sounded the same in bed. Not that she should be thinking about that. Somehow, she managed to keep up with him.

"Are you going easy on me?" she asked, panting.

"A little," he admitted.

"Well, don't."

Cooper sped up, and Sophie pushed herself to match him. The café came into view around the corner, perhaps two hundred meters away. She sprinted for the entrance, running purely on adrenaline. For a few seconds, she pulled ahead, but then Cooper broke away from her and she'd maxed out. He arrived at the café moments before she did.

Sophie leaned against the wall, letting it support her. "Thanks," she said once she could breathe again. "For not letting me win."

"I'm impressed," he told her. "I don't know many women who could give me a run for my money."

Sophie scoffed. "You probably know plenty of women who could if they tried, but they've got other things on their mind when you're with them."

Her eyes were teasing, and he responded in kind. "There's more than one kind of race, Shorty."

Sophie averted her eyes and shoved the door open with her shoulder. "You're such a *man*," she muttered.

"Still man-hating, are we?"

"Of course not. I'm over it." The words didn't quite ring true, but he didn't call her on it. "I broke up with Evan." Her romantic life probably didn't interest him, but tough luck. He was going to hear about it anyway. "For good this time. I think I want to be single for a while."

The thought of being single terrified her, but the thought of being stuck in another unfaithful relationship was worse. She couldn't handle that kind of pain.

"You're better off without him. I don't know what sort of man cheats on a girl like you, but he has to be a dumbass."

Sophie laughed. "Do you always say the right thing?"

"No," he said, his lips twitching at the corners. "The other night, I said all the wrong things."

"Mmm." Nodding, she studied the menu. "You're right, you did." The menu offered a berry smoothie, a green smoothie, and a tropical smoothie. "What's good?"

"The berry is my favorite," he told her.

"Two berry smoothies," she said decisively to the waitress.

They sat in a window booth. When the smoothies arrived, they were so pink that Sophie couldn't help teasing Cooper. "Not very manly, are they?"

"I disagree," he said, then slurped his smoothie in a way

that left a ring of foam around his mouth. "They're full of protein, antioxidants and fiber. Things that all manly men need."

"Whatever you say."

After they finished, they walked together until they reached Cooper's house.

"That was fun," Sophie said. "But let's have a few days of recovery time before we race again."

"Same time tomorrow?" he asked, humor twinkling in his eyes.

She swatted his arm. "I don't think I could survive."

"I'll see you then!" he called as she walked away.

Sophie smiled all the way home.

CHAPTER 3

Sophie wasted far too much of Sunday daydreaming about Cooper Simons. More specifically, about his bulging biceps, firm butt and muscular thighs. To distract herself, she guided Antonia through her muscle-strengthening exercises and told her about breaking up with Evan.

"He just hurt me too many times," she explained. "Cheating was the final straw. I don't suppose you'd know anything about that. You and Dad were always happy."

Antonia made a muffled noise and Sophie paused, trying to decipher whether it was a response to what she'd said, or a grunt of pain because she'd stretched beyond the comfortable limit. "What was that, Mum?"

"Always," Antonia murmured. "We were always happy."

Sophie relaxed and deepened the stretch. "I know you were," she assured her mother, then helped her into a different position. "I want what you had. But I've been thinking, just because I want that eventually doesn't mean I have to find it right now. I have time."

"You have plenty of time," Antonia said. "You're my daughter. You're beautiful."

Sophie smiled, heartened by how chatty her mother was,

even if she was delusional. "I've been thinking of taking some time off relationships to have a bit of fun."

Antonia didn't say anything, but her gaze settled on Sophie, and she seemed interested.

"Do you remember Cooper Simons?" Sophie asked. "Aria's brother?"

Antonia's eyes showed only confusion. She didn't reply, but that wasn't unusual. Multiple sclerosis had weakened the muscles she needed to talk, so verbalizing things could often require a lot of effort, and the words that emerged were slurred and difficult to understand.

"The middle kid," Sophie continued, manipulating Antonia's forearm. She'd become somewhat of an expert in these physical therapy routines since her mum had been diagnosed. "Justin is the older brother. He's the one with the curly hair you used to make fun of. Cooper is the younger one with blond hair who was always stealing your cookies."

She thought her mother nodded a little.

"Well, he's turned out pretty sexy." Sophie wasn't at all worried about sharing her thoughts with her mother. The only other person Antonia spoke to was Millicent, her nurse, and most of the time Millicent chattered while Antonia just absorbed the news of the outside world. "He's a total player, but I'm thinking of having an affair with him anyway. I know it's not usually my style, but you raised a modern woman, Mum. Anyway, I can separate sex from emotions, and he must be the same, or he wouldn't be able to go through as many women as he does. A fling with him might be exactly what I need to get over Evan."

"You want to use him."

Ouch. Was that censure in her mother's eyes? Or was she merely uncomfortable?

"I don't think he'll mind," Sophie said, easing back. "It'd be fun for both of us, so I see no reason for him to complain. We could use each other."

Antonia's forehead twitched. "What about Aria?"

"Aria wouldn't have to know. And if we both went into it expecting nothing more, then no one would get hurt."

"It's a bad idea."

Sophie chuckled and pressed a kiss to her mother's cheek. "You're a fine one to talk. You lost your heart and never took another chance with it again. You won't even leave the property to meet anyone new."

Antonia looked chastened, and Sophie immediately felt guilty for her comment, but she was forever hoping that something she said would prompt Antonia to put on one of the nice outfits she hadn't worn in years and brave the township. If only she weren't so damned proud. And if only she were less familiar with the gossipy nature of the locals.

"I love you," Sophie said. "You know that, right?"

Antonia's eyes watered.

"When you're ready to try, I'll be waiting for you."

She kissed her mother goodbye, then tucked the blankets around her body and removed the breakfast tray.

Cletus twined around her legs as she made the short walk back to her flat. The lights were off, unwashed clothing was scattered on the floor, and dust had settled on most of the surfaces. Sophie switched the light on, scooped Cletus into her arms and buried her face in his fur.

"You're so cute, kitty cat," she cooed. "Such a pretty boy."

Cletus purred loudly and arched towards her face, clearly agreeing with her. Giggling, she kissed the top of his furry head and put him down on the couch.

"I suppose I'd better clean up," she muttered. "You gonna help me, kitty?" Instead, he curled into a ball and started licking his paws. "Lazy cat. You're no help whatsoever."

BY EARLY AFTERNOON, Sophie had made a decision. Never one to spend days weighing pros and cons, she preferred to choose a course of action and go for it. She was going to ask Cooper to have a fling with her. But, although she was approaching it calmly, this was a situation she hadn't been in before. Usually, her relationships with men progressed naturally. She wasn't shy or afraid to ask for what she wanted, but in her experience, a certain degree of intimacy always preceded sex. If she got her way with Cooper, they'd progress from being acquaintances to friends to lovers in a matter of days. How lucky for her that he had no idea what she was planning, so he wouldn't be prepared when she struck.

She dressed to impress, pairing a tight tank top with dark jeans which could have been painted on. He had admired her legs, and she was going to make the most of that. She wasn't certain whether the attraction was mutual, but she'd approached men before and been rejected. This wouldn't be the first time she'd faced rejection, and it certainly wouldn't be the last, though it might be the most embarrassing, because she couldn't ignore him forever without raising some eyebrows. But that was something to deal with later on. Sophie was nothing if not single-minded.

You know, she thought, *this might be just the thing to help me get over Evan.*

Who better than a hot man to wipe another man from her mind? There had to be a limit on memories, right? All she had to do was knock all the Evan-related memories out of her brain and switch them for sexy Cooper-related memories. Then, maybe after Cooper, she'd find someone else to fill up her memories.

Sophie rubbed her palms together. This was beginning to sound like a very good idea indeed. Why hadn't she thought of it sooner?

There were plenty of good-looking guys in Itirangi other than Evan. Aria had snapped up one of them, but there were others. Sergeant Gareth Wayland was hot—although he was pining after Avery—but Doctor Ramsay Harding was easy on the eyes, too. Not to mention the dozens of strapping farmers who were in and out of town all the time. She wasn't vain enough to think she could have any of them, but certainly some of them would enjoy a casual fling. And if they were opposed at first, well, Sophie could be quite persuasive.

It was time to let loose again. She shouldn't dread being single; she should view it as an opportunity. Sophie was free to mingle and determined to enjoy it.

~

AFTER HIS RUN, Cooper showered and began developing photos in his darkroom. Photography was an occupation he'd taken up since his return from deployment. It wasn't particularly profitable, but he enjoyed it, and if the happy memories he recorded for other people didn't erase his own traumatic ones, they could at least distract him for a time.

Cooper used both digital and film photography, but he preferred doing it the old-fashioned way, spending peaceful time in his darkroom, surrounded by drying pictures. Wedding photography had its perks. Women loved weddings and got caught up in the excitement and romance. Bridesmaids were the best of the bunch, and more often than not, Cooper was invited to come home with one afterwards. It was an easy way to find women without dedicating too much time or effort to the task. All he needed to do was be charming, something he excelled at. He'd mastered the art at a young age, after he'd seen how Justin's bull-in-a-china-shop approach had gone down like a lead balloon with their parents.

He was hanging up a photo of a flower girl walking down the aisle when a knock sounded at the door. "Don't come in!"

he called, fearing his photos would be compromised. "I'll be out in a moment."

After he'd finished up, he untied the apron from his waist and exited through the rear door, which was arranged to block out all light. To his surprise, Sophie was hovering in his hallway. She'd changed since earlier and looked more like herself.

His gaze slid leisurely down her body. Her toned legs were encased in denim, and the tank top which hugged her torso left little to the imagination. He'd been shocked to find himself checking her out earlier and had wondered at the time if it was a result of his new conviction not to sleep with anyone. He decided that might have been partially the case, but she still attracted him now. He imagined pressing her supple body against the wall, and grimaced when his lower half stirred. She didn't have much going on in the breast department, but that didn't bother him. He'd always been more of a leg man.

"Hey." She greeted him with a warm smile, as if they hadn't seen each other only a couple of hours ago.

He returned her smile. "To what do I owe the pleasure?"

Sophie shifted from one foot to the other and glanced towards the living room. "Can we sit down?"

"Yeah, sure."

Contrary to popular belief, Cooper didn't often have women in his house, preferring instead to go to their places. Nevertheless, the fridge was always stocked with lemonade, just in case. After helping himself to a can, he lobbed another one across the room, and was impressed when she caught it without fumbling. She was nervous, he realized as he sat next to her, but he couldn't imagine why.

"I have a proposition," she blurted, studying the can without opening it, and avoiding his gaze.

"Yes?" he asked.

"I think we should have a fling."

Cooper didn't understand. "A fling?"

Her cheeks grew red, and he knew that despite her bravado, this was hard for her to say.

"As in, an affair. Casual sex. I would like someone to have sex with, no strings attached."

He was stuck between laughing and swearing. "And you thought of me?"

"You're a playboy," she said, as if that explained it all. "I want hot sex without any expectations. That seems like something you'd be into."

Cooper's groin tightened at hearing the words 'hot sex' come from the mouth of a woman with whom he would be extremely interested in doing just that—under different circumstances. "But you're Aria's friend."

"She wouldn't have to know." Sophie spoke decisively. "It would be for a set amount of time. A few days or a couple of weeks, at most. Just to work it out of my system. I've had casual sex before, and so have you. It wouldn't need to be a big deal."

She'd had casual sex before? That was news to him. Not that he'd paid much attention to any of Aria's friends, but he had always assumed they were as virtuous as his sister. It seemed he'd been mistaken.

"Sweetheart," he said, "I'd love to take you up on your offer, but you're my sister's friend, and it would muddy the waters. It's a bad idea."

"Oh." Sophie cracked open her lemonade, sipped it, and let the silence draw out for a minute. "I guess I'd better find someone else, then."

"Yeah, you... Wait, what?"

"I need sex, Coop."

If someone had said a week ago that he'd be hearing those words come from Sophie Delaware's mouth, he'd have told them they were bat-shit crazy. He was so far out of his depth, it was laughable. "So... What?"

"So, I'll find someone else." Standing, she drained the can of lemonade, then dropped it on the table. "Thanks for the drink."

"Who else will you find?" he asked, leaping out of his chair and following her to the door. "You can't just have sex with a stranger, Soph."

Sophie laughed and rolled her eyes. "I won't, don't worry. I know enough men who'll jump at the offer of sex that I won't have to resort to strangers." She paused, nibbling on her lower lip. "I'm sorry if that was awkward for you."

"Forget about it," he said, but she'd already left.

Cooper went back to the couch and collapsed, his mind whirling with confusion. What the hell had just happened?

A WEEK LATER, Cooper headed to Aria's place for dinner. He wished he could talk to his brother or sister about his odd encounter with Sophie the previous weekend, but he didn't want to face their shock or censure. Surely, he had done the right thing by turning her down. The responsible thing. He couldn't sleep with Aria's friends. There were rules about things like that. They weren't written down, but they were understood. It was like dating a friend's ex: you just didn't do it.

But then, Sophie was a grown woman. A sexy woman. She could make up her own mind. And he was a grown man. He didn't need permission from his little sister to have a tussle in bed with a willing woman. But then, this wasn't just any willing woman. It was Sophie. Of all her friends, Aria was most protective of Sophie, who wasn't as beautiful as Clarissa, as practical as Avery, or as easy-come-easy-go as Evie.

She was Sophie, a complex woman with complex needs.

Damn it all to hell. He wouldn't have known any of this if

it weren't for her friendship with Aria, which was exactly the reason he couldn't sleep with her. Cooper preferred his women to be strangers he could remove from his life as soon as it suited him. Yes, it was cold of him, but also convenient.

What confused him most was why was he couldn't stop agonizing over his decision. He'd refused, and she'd accepted it graciously. Far too graciously, in his opinion. It would have been nice if she had seemed a little put out by his rejection. But no, she'd calmly moved on to the next guy on her list. *Who was he?* Cooper wondered. This backup guy couldn't possibly be aware of the trouble he was about to find himself in. Make no mistake, this new version of Sophie couldn't bring anything but trouble. Unfortunately, it seemed unlikely that any other man would turn her down. Cooper had to; he had no choice in the matter. But other men wouldn't be bound by the same constrictions, and they would certainly take her up on her offer.

Then what?

What does it matter? It doesn't.

THERE'D BEEN a time when visiting Aria's house for Saturday dinner was routine for Sophie, but she'd stopped after she began dating Evan. Once, she'd made the mistake of bringing him along, hoping her friends would take to him, but it had been a flop. A completely tragic flop. In the space of two hours, he'd offered Aria cooking advice (an ill-advised move), asked Justin about his relationship status (recently dumped), and done the same for Cooper (a serial dater). Then he'd made a derogatory comment about military men having a girl in every port. It had been meant as a joke, but Cooper was proud of his time in the service and took comments like that to heart. While Evan hadn't directly offended Mr. or Mrs. Simons, they'd disliked him on behalf of their children.

The only person he hadn't upset was Avery, who was immune to personal jabs and had decided early on that he was a tool and not worth bothering with. Sophie had been so embarrassed, she hadn't gone again. Now that she was done with Evan—and she truly was—she was free to spend time with her friends without worrying what Evan might do or say next. Her relief was palpable.

She was especially keen to go tonight because she owed Cooper an apology. Playboy or not, it wasn't fair to proposition him without any warning. Considering she was his sister's friend, she'd put him in an awkward situation, and he had responded remarkably well. The sharp twinge of pain she'd felt when he'd turned her down hurt, but in a way, she'd expected it, so her reply had been smooth and casual, better than she could have hoped for. But no matter how maturely they had handled the encounter, she should clear the air between them so there would be no need to treat each other cautiously in the future.

Sophie arrived at Aria's home twenty minutes before dinner was due to start, armed with a cake of chocolate. Aria enveloped her in a hug, and for the first time, Sophie felt the curve of her three-months-pregnant belly.

"Hi, bubba!" she cooed, speaking to the baby bump. "I'm your aunty Sophie. I can't wait to meet you."

Aria rolled her eyes and snatched the chocolate. "Not you, too."

Eli chuckled, and Sophie glanced over to see him standing in the corner. "It's important for Lauren to know her dad's voice," he said, smiling tenderly at Aria.

Sophie felt a pang of longing for an Eli of her own. Well, not an Eli, precisely, but someone who would look at her that way and believe the sun rose and set because of her. With a conscious effort, she discarded the thought. There was no Eli for her. No romance-of-a-lifetime. But it didn't matter. She could have a rich and full life anyway.

"So, it's a girl?" she asked.

Aria and Eli exchanged glances. "We don't know."

"We've decided to wait to find out," Aria explained. "Well, Eli decided. I wanted to know—"

"But *I* thought it would make it more special to wait," Eli finished for her. "I'm hoping for a girl."

"But I want a little boy who will be just like his daddy."

"You two are disgustingly cute," Sophie complained, inviting herself inside and sitting on a worn chair. "I don't know whether to poke my eyes out or eat you up."

"I'd rather neither," Eli replied, crossing the room to wrap an arm around his woman.

"Poke your eyes out," Teri said, emerging from the hall. "Definitely. And can you poke mine out while you're at it? I love them, but they're sickening."

Sophie laughed. She loved the teenager's sass. But instead of being drawn into a cycle of sarcasm, she changed the topic. "Who all's coming tonight?"

Aria stepped away and stirred a pot on the stove. "As far as I know, Mum and Dad, Justin and Emily, Avery and Cooper."

Sophie didn't like the way Aria had paired Cooper with Avery. She knew it wasn't intentional—that as the only two single people coming, it made sense to lump them together, but it rubbed her the wrong way. *Stop it,* she chided herself. He was her friend's older brother, nothing more. But how she wished he could be more.

Justin arrived with Emily soon after. They were a lovely couple. Though they'd only recently announced their relationship, they'd been dating in secrets for months—or so they'd thought. Most of the town had known long before they made it public.

Emily's cheeks were flushed from happiness and the first blush of love. Justin was his usual cranky self, but his hard edges were beginning to soften. He congratulated Sophie on the end of her relationship with an egomaniac, but despite his gruffness, his brow was furrowed with concern and she knew that he worried about her. She shook her head and shrugged. She didn't know what to say, but it seemed to satisfy him.

Cooper arrived just before the dinner was dished. Sophie tried not to look as if she'd been waiting for him all night. *You're apologizing,* she told herself. *Nothing else.* His eyes widened when he saw her seated at the table, and she smiled tentatively. While they ate, she kept her eyes on her food and tried to join the conversation often enough for no one to notice how preoccupied she was.

When the meal was finished and Emily started clearing away the dishes, Sophie snagged Cooper by the elbow and led him outside. They walked to the far end of the garden, where they were partially shielded by bushes.

"What's up?" Cooper asked, gently removing her hand from his elbow.

"I want to say sorry," Sophie explained. "I'm not usually so forward, and I didn't mean to put you in an awkward spot. Are we all right? No weirdness?"

"No weirdness," Cooper confirmed with a warm smile. "You worry too much, Soph."

"Thanks." She turned to go back inside, but his hand on her waist stopped her. When she met his eyes, they flared with more than friendship.

"Just so you know, if you weren't Aria's friend, I would have taken you up on your offer in a heartbeat."

Sophie's stomach leapt into her throat, and she stuttered a bunch of meaningless syllables. "You would?"

"Yes." His fingers tightened on her waist. "As you've pointed out, I'm a connoisseur of women, and you are a very desirable woman."

His blue eyes were so dark, Sophie thought she could swim in them. His breath hitched, drawing her attention to his lips. They were full for a man, kissable. How she wished he would kiss her.

"Sophie, don't look at me like that," he groaned.

"Like what?" she whispered.

"Like you want me to kiss you."

"I do," she confessed. "I've been thinking about it all week."

"You don't make it easy for a guy to be noble."

"I prefer men who take what they want," Sophie admitted, her tongue so thick that she tripped over the words. It was her darkest fantasy to be utterly possessed by a man, to have him take what he wanted from her without so much as asking. She'd never been brave enough to approach such a man, or enact her fantasy, but she was certain that Cooper could be just the man for the job.

It seemed she might be right. His eyes turned molten, as if he could read her mind, and he curved his other hand around her waist, pulling her into the shelter of his body. His hands cupped her bottom as he pressed her closer, his heat radiating out to encompass her. There was a brief pause while they looked into each other's eyes—checking for second thoughts—then Cooper's delectably kissable lips descended onto hers.

Sophie stretched onto her toes, pressing herself against him, sliding her body against his. His tongue swept over her lips, and she opened them, letting him into her mouth. It was the hottest invasion she'd ever experienced. If this was what kissing him felt like, what would it feel like to do more?

Stop fantasizing!

Cooper's big hands moved up her body to cover her breasts, and a zing of awareness shot through her when one of his fingers massaged a circle over her nipple. Sophie gasped into his mouth. The sound seemed to inflame him, and he squeezed her nipple to make her do it again. Crying out softly, she ran her hands down his back, feeling the strength of his body. He shifted his hands to her butt and lifted her, carried her a few yards away to a tree and pinned her against it. With the rough bark against her back and a hot male pressed to her front, Sophie thought she might be in heaven, and Cooper was as aroused as she. The bulge in his jeans couldn't be concealed, and she rocked her hips against it, eliciting from him a low groan.

"You are so hot," he said, his voice rough with desire. "This is so wrong."

"It doesn't have to be." She was dizzy with want.

He drew back slightly and pressed his forehead to hers. "I don't do relationships."

"Good thing I'm only looking for fun."

He pecked her lips. "I'm a fun guy."

Sophie's eyes twinkled, and she tipped her chin up. "Then, what's the problem?"

"What problem?" Cooper claimed her lips in a slow kiss, then broke away, cursing. "If we keep this up, our first time is going to be here on Aria's lawn."

"You're right. We need to slow this down."

He set her on her feet, and she stumbled. He caught her by the waist and steadied her.

"Tonight," she murmured in his ear. "My place. After this."

She thought he might refuse—a last-ditch attempt to be honorable—but he smiled wickedly and cupped her buttocks, pulling her more tightly against his body.

"I'll be there."

CHAPTER 4

The moment she arrived home, Sophie darted around collecting pieces of clothing to shove in the wardrobe, moving the stack of unwashed dishes from her bedroom and vacuuming cat fur off the bed sheets. No one visited her cottage, so she didn't usually worry about keeping it tidy. As a result, most of the surfaces were strewn with clothing, books and cosmetic tubes.

"What a pig sty," she exclaimed, closing her eyes in the hope that it might all disappear and leave a sophisticated bachelorette pad behind. Jeez, if the mess was enough to turn Sophie off, what effect would it have on Cooper? Well, she wasn't going to find out.

She hurried out to check on Antonia, who was sleeping soundly, then fed Cletus and locked him on the other side of the living room door, along with the mess. Thankfully, her bedroom was near the front door, so Cooper wouldn't need to see the disaster zone in the rest of the house. Except... The bathroom. Panicking, Sophie ran into the bathroom and gasped in horror. Makeup containers covered the vanity. The only exposed surface was dusted by a fine layer of brown powder—possibly bronzer. She clicked the containers shut, threw them inside the vanity and wiped the top clean with a cloth, then hauled the overflowing laundry basket down the hall and shut it behind the living room door, out of sight.

Finally, she took a breath and looked around. Her bedroom was passably tidy and the bathroom passably clean. It could be seen as the home of a human being rather than a rampaging wildebeest.

She glanced at herself in the mirror and froze. She looked like she'd run a marathon, then rolled around in the dirt. Not a look she wanted when she had an assignation with one of the most desirable men she'd ever met. She wanted to look her goddamn best.

She turned the shower on and jumped in while it was still cold, swearing violently. Not her best idea. Taking care not to get her hair wet lest she have to blow-dry it—which inevitably quadrupled its volume—she lathered herself in soap and ran a razor over her legs. She dried quickly and rubbed moisturizer on, then applied a minimal amount of makeup—mascara, eye shadow, concealer—so she looked good but natural. She took care to emphasize her eyes; they were her best feature. Then she raided her drawers, searching for the right outfit. After quickly dismissing the one she had worn to meet Evan, she chose a pale pink slip with a matching silk thong. She'd just dressed when her doorbell rang.

Taking a deep breath to calm her racing heart, and trying to look as cool as a cucumber, she opened the door. Cooper was standing at the threshold, taking up most of the doorway. His thumbs were hooked through his belt loops and he looked immensely confident, as if he often called on women late at night. Which he probably did. His eyes widened when he saw her, and then his gaze slid appreciatively down her body and back up to meet her eyes.

"You look good."

The low timbre of his voice sent goosebumps racing over

Sophie's exposed skin. Her physical reaction to him didn't go unnoticed. He stepped forward and grabbed her arms. His hands were so large, they almost covered her forearms. Sexy hands. Even though she knew it was weird, Sophie had a thing for hands. She liked big, rough hands because they made her feel small and delicate. She shivered beneath his touch.

"Are you sure about this?" he asked, stepping even closer so that their bodies almost touched, aligned in all the good places.

Sophie longed to close the gap between them. The air was buzzing with sexual tension. "Absolutely."

There could be no regrets about spending time with such a potent man. He dragged her to him, and their lips met hard enough to knock Sophie back a step, but then she softened. He responded by gentling his kiss, his lips coaxing and sweet.

Why did he have to be so perfect? She could easily imagine becoming addicted to this man. It wasn't too late to change her mind, and logically she knew she ought to do just that, but damn it, she deserved to be naughty for a while. She wasn't the cover girl for good behavior, but she'd earned a bit of fun.

Drawing back, she bit her lip and smiled at him shyly. "Come into the bedroom."

THE MOMENT she uttered those words, Cooper knew he was lost. He'd fought his reaction when he opened the door to see her in a skimpy nighty and tiny underwear, her glorious legs completely bare and her small breasts propped up by a Wonderbra, her complexion like peaches and cream. It had taken every bit of his self-restraint not to ravish her on the spot. Instead, he took his time. But when she invited him into her bedroom, the wild beast inside him reared its head.

He couldn't believe he was reacting to her so strongly. Kissing her in his sister's garden had made him harder than he'd been outside of the bedroom in years. He felt like a randy teenager who couldn't keep it together. Now, he gave in to his baser instincts and scooped her off her feet with one arm, curving his other hand around her breast. God, it was great how easily he could take her weight. He'd never realized the benefits of making love to a small woman. He used to think of Sophie as childlike, but that was definitely not the case, and with her being so small, he could reposition her as it suited him. A host of ideas ran through his mind at the thought.

Sophie swung her legs around Cooper's waist and dug her heels into his muscular thighs. She loved the sensation of being overwhelmed by him. Her movement brought her core into contact with the hard ridge beneath his jeans, and a burst of pleasure shot through her as she rubbed herself against him. The friction of denim on bare skin was exquisite. Air hissed between his teeth, then in two strides he was inside the bedroom and shoving the door shut, pinning her against it.

They stayed joined at the mouth, and Sophie rocked against him, trying to get some relief from the pressure building at her core.

"Oh, God," he groaned into her mouth. "You're such a tease."

Sophie laughed breathlessly. "It's not teasing if I let you have me."

Cooper's hard shaft pulsed at her words. "Do you know what you do to me?"

She nipped the skin at his neck and reveled in the shudder that ripped through him. "I hope it's good."

She wriggled against him, and the air whooshed out of her lungs when he deposited her on the bed so he could tug his shirt over his head. Holy hell, he was gorgeous. His chest was broad, with defined pecs, and his abs were perfect ripples of muscle covered by tan skin, marred only by a white scar that stood out starkly against his golden complexion.

Sophie's mouth went dry. Her fingers twitched towards him, seeming to act of their own free will, and she came to the edge of the bed to stroke his abs, pleased when he sucked in another breath and closed his eyes. Fascinated by his astounding muscle definition, she lowered her head and tasted his chest, trailing her lips and tongue along his pec and up to his nipple, which she rolled beneath her tongue. This magnificent man was hers to explore.

"That's enough," he said, his voice rough.

Surprised, she looked up into blazing eyes that made her toes curl with desire. Feeling bold, she traced a finger along the waistband of his jeans and then slipped it inside.

"I don't think so."

She took him in her hands, marveling at the heat and size of him. There might be more than one reason why the ladies loved Cooper. Closing her fist over him, she pumped her hand slowly, her movements restricted by the fitted denim. With her free hand, she unzipped his jeans and pushed them down, maintaining her rhythm while he kicked them and his briefs away impatiently.

"You're pushing your luck," he ground out, squeezing his eyes tightly closed.

Sophie bent to lick his shaft, and his hips jerked. Then he lifted her by her upper arms and carried her to the dressing table, cleared it with a sweep of his arm, and sat her down. The wood was cool on her bottom, but Cooper was hot between her thighs. There was a snap, and he cast her underwear aside, the flimsy fabric torn apart. Taking her mouth, he swallowed her whimper as he covered her center with a hand, slipping a finger between the folds of her sex. His finger rubbed along her slit while his palm cupped her, and pleasure grew within her. Finally, the finger slipped inside her, and it was almost too much.

"Please," Sophie gasped.

"Please, what?"

He wanted her to beg? She wasn't above begging. "Please, Coop," she cried. "I need you inside me."

"This might hurt," he said harshly, after he'd slid on a condom and positioned himself at her entrance. "You're so small."

Sophie wrapped her legs around his hips and pulled him towards her. He was a large man in every way, but she wanted all of him. "I can take you, Coop," she said. "Don't hold back. I want it."

He surged inside her, and she bit down on a scream. He stiffened. "Did that hurt?" His body was tense, thrumming with desire. "I can stop if you need me to."

In answer, Sophie drew his mouth to hers and kissed him, their tongues twining together as she shuffled her hips forward to encourage his thrusts. At first he moved slowly, and she was delirious with pleasure, but her moans and gasps urged him on, and his movements became frenzied.

SHE FELT SO good wrapped around him. So warm and slick. Cooper had thought to get revenge for her teasing by making her desperate for him, but she'd embraced the sweet torture, which only made him crazier for her.

He hadn't been disappointed. Being inside of her was the most pleasurable torment he'd ever experienced. Sophie's lithe body was crushed against his, and he wanted to get closer and closer.

"Cooper," she gasped as her hips twitched. "So good."

He could feel himself losing control but held on to that last fraying bit of restraint. Then her hands gripped his ass and her internal muscles clenched around him. His pelvis ground into her most sensitive part, and she shuddered deliciously. The sensation of her soft walls clamping around him was too much for Cooper, and he let go, pumping into her one last time and groaning in ecstasy.

~

SOPHIE'S HEAD rested on Cooper's chest as she caught her breath, a massive grin spreading across her face. His chest heaved beneath her cheek, and his chin dug into the top of her head as his breath rasped in and out. He was still inside her, and Sophie had no desire for him to leave. It was just as she had expected: hands down, the most spectacular sex of her life. She'd be a happy woman if she could do it again and again and again.

"That was..." She trailed off as her mind failed to come up with an adequate descriptor.

"It was," he agreed.

Their bodies were beginning to cool but were still slippery with sweat as he carefully pulled away from her. His hands on her hips, he lowered her to the floor on legs so weak that she was amazed they didn't fold beneath her weight. She stumbled over the edge of the rug, but his muscular arms supported her so there was no danger of falling. Cooper didn't release her until she was seated on the edge of the bed, studying his magnificent body.

He was gorgeous. Pure masculine perfection.

"You should always be naked," Sophie declared. "Naked suits you."

Cooper chuckled as he retrieved his jeans from the floor and stepped into them, the waistband slung low around his hips as he zipped it up. The motion drew her eye to the ragged scar that crossed his stomach from left hip to the right side of his rib cage. She wondered if it was a souvenir from his days in the navy. Such a wound must have been horribly painful, even life-threatening.

"I could say the same for you," he said.

Sophie rolled her eyes. "I'm serious. It's like you've been sculpted from marble."

That sounded stupid, but she couldn't help it. The only places she'd ever seen men like him were in movies and on the internet, certainly not semi-naked in her bedroom. This was the stuff of her fantasies.

She stifled a giggle. Cooper was going to bring her fantasies to life, and he didn't even know it. Then she frowned. He didn't seem as willing to comply as she'd hoped, having managed to slip into his shirt while Sophie was preoccupied. Now he was tying his shoelaces.

What about round two?

She was ready for round two. Rounds three, four and five as well. In fact, she'd go as many more rounds as Cooper was up for. Which was, apparently, none. What sort of playboy loved and left this soon? *Okaaay, stupid question.* But surely he'd want as much easy sex as he could get before he moved on.

"Thanks, Soph." Cooper kissed her on the cheek, avoiding her mouth when she turned toward him. *Wow, way to make a girl feel like your sister.* "That was incredible."

"You're not staying?" She couldn't help feeling disappointed.

He looked pained. Was she being overly clingy? Self-doubt began to creep into her mind. With Evan in her life, it had been a while since she'd had a fling. Maybe she'd lost the knack.

"There's something we should get straight right now," Cooper said. "I don't sleep with women, ever." His face grew serious, and he wouldn't make eye contact with her. "I have sex, make love, screw, fuck, whatever you want to call it. I give pleasure and take it, but I don't sleep with anyone. If we want to keep this casual, I need to play by the same rules I always do."

"That's fine." She did her best to sound flippant, although getting lumped in with other women hurt. She preferred to think of the two of them and the amazing time they'd had together, and not of anything else. "You're completely right. I'll see you again, though?"

"Of course."

He smiled and pulled his hair back into a ponytail, eyes twinkling. Combined with his sharp cheekbones and strong jaw, the effect was devastating. Sophie sucked in a breath. She was so far out of her depth.

"Two weeks," she blurted.

"What?"

A flush worked its way up her chest, staining her pale skin pink. "Our affair should have an end date. Two weeks. That way, we both know when it's going to end, and there's no awkwardness or expectations." Any longer than two weeks, and she would lose her heart. With rock star good looks, a wicked smile and clever hands, Cooper posed a danger to her peace of mind.

"You're so eager to get away from me?"

His tone was teasing, and Sophie couldn't help but smile. "Not so eager. But you're going to leave me, so I need to set some ground rules."

Standing, still naked, Sophie pressed herself against Cooper's body. "I understand that you need to go, but I want you to know that I'm going to be in your bed as much as you'll let me for the next two weeks. I hope you can keep up." She slicked an open-mouthed kiss across his lips and winked. Then she shoved his shoulders. "Now, off with you."

Cooper grasped her upper arms and dipped his face to hers. "I accept your challenge."

The kiss grew heated quickly, and Sophie was glad to have support from the bed behind her. Groaning against her mouth, he rubbed his tongue along hers and drew back reluctantly.

"I never imagined..." he murmured, "how passionate you would be. How responsive."

His finger trailed along her chin, and Sophie closed her eyes, reveling in his touch. When his finger stopped on her lip, she sucked it into her mouth.

"Sophie."

Meeting his eyes, all innocence, Sophie raised an eyebrow.

Cooper reclaimed his finger and frowned. "If you keep doing that, I'm going to pin you to the bed and ravish you so thoroughly, you won't be able to walk in the morning."

Her heart thumped in her chest. Could she really have such an effect on this powerful man? "Yes, please."

Cooper laughed. "You're insatiable."

"Yes, I am." Sophie had never been ashamed of her sexual appetite. She'd never had any complaints.

"I'm going now," he said. "Before you tear my clothes off again."

Feeling wonderfully bubbly and light, despite being unable to stop him from leaving, Sophie shrugged into her silk robe and led him to the door.

"Let's do this again," she suggested.

"Same time tomorrow?"

"I can't wait."

Cooper let himself out, and Sophie watched him saunter to his truck with a slow, swinging stride. The man was utterly delicious. With a big grin plastered on her face, she sighed like a schoolgirl as she closed the door and leaned against it.

The clock on the hallway wall said it was just before 10 p.m., early enough to take her mother a late-night snack. Sophie prepared a tray of cheese and crackers and walked the path to the main house.

Antonia had woken since Sophie had last checked on her. Sitting on the edge of the bed, Sophie held a cracker in front of her mother's lips and helped her eat it.

"I have such a story for you," she said. "You know I was thinking of having an affair with Cooper Simons?" Antonia didn't respond, but Sophie carried on regardless. "Well, it's happening. And, oh man. He is ah-may-zing. Just what I need."

Antonia blinked and stared her down.

"Yes, yes, I know you disapprove. But, Mum, the chemistry is great, and he's so much fun. I promise I'll be safe. I'll let you know how it goes."

CHAPTER 5

The fierce Iranian sun beat down on Cooper's back as he and Second Lieutenant Ben Macintosh walked back to their military vehicle to return to the HMS Canterbury *after visiting a base camp.*

Everything in Iran seemed to be some shade of brown or yellow. The earth, the buildings, even the air appeared as a haze of dust. Cooper couldn't wait to see the end of it. Home was lush and green, quiet and peaceful. If he made it back, he swore he'd find a girl and settle down the way his parents wanted him to. He would coach rugby and learn to be an accountant, a builder, or something else suitably low-risk. Not that Cooper liked low-risk. He lived for the thrill of his work, the danger and the brotherhood. But he was sick of the goddamn brown-ness of it all.

Ben voiced his thoughts. "Two months, and we'll be back in New Zealand. Can't wait to get out of this godforsaken place."

"Not long now," Cooper agreed. His six-year contract was almost at an end, and he wouldn't be signing up for another stint as a first lieutenant aboard the HMS Canterbury. *Six years was enough time in service of his country. Patriotism still flared red-hot in his veins, but it was time to express it in other ways. His parents*

were getting older, and his sister was twenty-one now. She'd been in high school the last time he'd seen her.

The military kept sending him to more dangerous places. Cooper had a reputation for being lucky, but everyone's luck ran out eventually, and he'd rather be in a safe environment when that happened.

Ben had a girlfriend and a daughter to return to. He and Cooper had joined the navy at the same time. Now, Ben was counting the days until he could be with his girls.

"How are Trisha and Madison?" Cooper asked.

Ben pulled his cell phone from his pocket and scrolled through, stopping at a photo of an attractive brunette holding a chubby-cheeked baby.

"Trisha sent this last week," he replied.

Cooper smiled. "You're a lucky man. How did you convince Trisha she couldn't do any better than your ugly mug?"

"I put a remotely activated rifle in her bedroom. Took out the competition."

"Good thinking."

Ben chucked the keys to Cooper, who caught them easily. "Your turn."

Cooper pressed the lock release button, and the world exploded around them.

The roar was so loud, it filled Cooper's ears even after it had stopped. Then the ringing began, a piercing squeal that rose in volume and pitch until it was unbearable. Dust and debris clouded the air. His vision faded in and out, blinding white spots dancing in front of his eyes. The world seemed to rotate by 90 degrees, the ground becoming vertical and everything else spinning around him.

Cooper put his hands on the ground and pushed himself upright, putting the sky back in the right place. His nerve endings were screaming, and when he brought his hands to his face, they were shaking and covered with warm, sticky blood.

He looked down. The front of his uniform was stained scarlet, and it might have been all that was holding him together.

Ben. Where was Ben?

Crawling through the debris from the car, Cooper made his way to his friend. Ben was in worse shape than Cooper, sprawled on the ground, blood pooling beneath his head. Cooper summoned a burst of strength and hauled him into a sitting position, propping him against a door panel. The man's eyes were unfocussed.

"Ben!" he yelled, unable to hear himself over the shrieking in his ears. "Get it together!"

Ben slowly turned toward him. "Coop?"

"Yeah." Cooper felt a rush of relief. "We've been hit."

Ben's eyes rolled back in his head.

"Stay with me, man. Stay with me."

Often, head wounds weren't as severe as they appeared. Cooper ripped off his torn sleeve and used it to apply pressure to Ben's wound. Ben was concussed, that was all. He'd be fine.

Cooper slapped his cheek. "Don't sleep! Stay awake, Lieutenant. That's an order."

Ben's eyes focused again. "T-t-t-," he stuttered. Cooper leaned closer to hear him. "T-Trish..."

"Trisha is fine," Cooper assured him. "So is Madison. They're waiting for you at home, buddy."

"T-t-take care..."

"We're fine. The bomb is finished. We're okay."

"...of Trisha."

"I don't need to, Ben. You're gonna go home and take care of her yourself."

His friend met his eyes, and Cooper knew he wasn't much longer for the world. Whatever Cooper might say, Ben wasn't going to see Trisha and Madison again.

"T-take care."

"I will," he promised. "I'll find them, and I'll look after them."

Ben's hand fumbled, and Cooper watched as he struggled to find his cell phone and shove it into Cooper's pocket.

"My gun." His voice was thready, barely there.

Cooper grabbed the gun, lying a couple of feet away, and curled Ben's fingers around it. Then he clapped it to his chest.

"Hooyah," Ben whispered.

"Hooyah," Cooper replied.

Then Ben's eyes drifted closed, and Cooper was left alone in hostile land with the corpse of his best friend, surely bleeding internally and waiting for backup to arrive.

He drifted away and didn't wake for two days.

COOPER WOKE as he bolted upright, drenched in sweat. His heart was racing, and his ears were ringing from a blast that had happened more than four years ago.

"Fuck," he swore, covering his eyes with a damp palm and drawing in shaky breaths that rattled through his chest.

As usual, nothing more than a sheet covered him, and now it was soaked through. A clean sheet lay folded on the cabinet next to him. He would replace the bedding as soon as he could bring himself to crawl out of bed and face the world. He couldn't stay here after having the dream; he was too afraid of falling asleep and going through it all over again.

Stupid, really. Nearly every night, he experienced the same dream and woke to face another day. Despite that, he managed to be in good spirits. After all, what did he have to mope about? He was twenty-nine years old, in the best condition of his life, with a job he enjoyed and an endless stream of women eager to share his bed. Not that they ever did. At least, not overnight. He couldn't bear for anyone to witness his night terrors. It had been bad enough when he was freshly home from Iran and everyone seemed to watch him with a combination of pity and wariness.

As he was the only veteran in Itirangi to have served overseas within the past two decades, no one had been sure how to behave around him. Everyone felt sorry for him, of course. People liked to feel sorry for veterans. But they were distrustful, too. While PTSD campaigns were supposed to bring attention to the suffering of veterans, they inadvertently gave people the idea that he might break down at any moment. That he might become emotionally overwrought, cowering in fear from everyday noises, or break with reality and become dangerous.

The rumors weren't entirely false. It had taken months of training before Cooper could remain composed when a car backfired or a child shrieked with laughter. He'd become a playboy to give the busybodies something else to gossip about. With a mixture of determination and good acting, Cooper had ensured that no one knew he woke up in a cold sweat every night, his dead friend's face imprinted on his mind. To them, he seemed normal. He liked it that way.

The alarm went off. Cooper swatted the clock off the bedside table—a daily routine—and threw the sheet back. After a brief shower, he tore the used sheets from the bed, spread new ones on, and jogged out the door.

No sign of Sophie this morning. Cooper had to admit he was disappointed. They'd ended their tryst on such good terms that, try as he might to deny it, he couldn't wait to see her again. Who knew she'd be such a spitfire? God, the way she'd responded to him had been incredible, and to hear her begging for him... Well, Cooper went hard again just thinking about it. He'd hoped to encounter her during his run, but luck wasn't on his side.

Was she avoiding him? Or perhaps he'd worn her out and she was in bed recovering. A smug smirk tugged at his lips. Now, that was more like it.

After running until his legs were burning, Cooper drove twenty-five minutes north towards the coast and stopped outside a weatherboard cottage. The front yard was manicured, with alternating pink and white roses bordering both the cottage and a knee-high brick wall. Cooper knew the back section had enough room to kick a soccer ball and a paved barbecue area complete with outdoor table and cane chairs. It was a working-class family's dream.

Knocking on the front door, he wondered whether he should have brought a box of chocolates. He often found himself outside Trisha's door after a particularly rough night. She seemed to understand and didn't judge him for it.

The door swung open, and Trisha beamed at him, stepping forward to wrap her arms around him.

"It's great to see you, Cooper!" she exclaimed, rubbing her palms along his upper arms soothingly as she stretched up to kiss his cheek. "How are you?"

"Same as ever," he replied. "Getting through."

Trisha nodded. She understood all about getting though things. "Why don't you come in?"

The top of the door frame was only an inch above his head as Cooper walked into the cottage. The smell of bacon was wafting down the hall, and a radio was playing in the kitchen. A girl was sitting at the table, small for a five-year-old. Petite and blonde, sure to be a heartbreaker one day. A plate of partially eaten bacon had been pushed precariously close to the edge of the table to make way for a My Little Pony board game.

Madison raised her head and squealed at the sight of him.

"Uncle Coop!" she cried as he swept her into a hug, lifting her feet off the floor.

"If it's not my little Maddy," he grinned, swinging her in an arc before lowering her back into her seat. "Your mummy tells me she's beating you at My Little Pony. Is that true?"

He enjoyed her horrified expression as she turned to Trisha and gasped, "You are *not*!"

Trisha shrugged.

"But I *won.*"

"There's only one way to prove it," Cooper said, speaking slowly and thoughtfully, the little girl hanging on his every word. "You're going to have to beat *both* of us. Do you think you can do that?"

Maddy nodded eagerly. Trisha rolled her eyes.

Cooper felt at ease for the first time that morning. "Then let's play."

SOPHIE MANAGED NOT to call Cooper for most of the day. At five o'clock, she'd finished work, and because it was apparent by then that he wouldn't be calling her, she caved. Of course, they'd planned to meet that evening, but she didn't know what time, or what to expect. He'd seemed pretty pleased last night, but what if he hadn't enjoyed their time together as much as she had? What if he was having second thoughts?

The call went straight to voicemail and she sighed, debating whether to leave a message and feel pathetic, or hang up and wonder all evening whether she should have left a message. Then the beep sounded, and she made a decision.

"Hey, Coop," she whispered in her best seductive voice, which might also have sounded as if she were having an asthma attack. Difficult to know. "It's Sophie, here. I had a really good time last night. I can't wait to do it all again. I'll see you later."

Then she hit the end button and took a deep breath. *Play it cool, Soph.*

She and Cooper were two consenting adults who didn't have to be in each other's pockets. They'd slept together once, that was it. They weren't dating.

The phone rang shrilly, and she twitched in surprise, then quickly accepted the call and pressed the phone to her ear.

"Hello," she said breathlessly.

"Sophie!" an excited voice cried. Definitely not Cooper. Too high-pitched, too excited, too *female*. She checked the caller ID. Of course.

"Evie!" she squealed back. "How are you? It's so good to hear from you."

"I have something for you," Evie sang in her odd, husky voice, which Sophie had always been jealous of. It was earthy and sensual. And by God, Evie could sing like a wonder.

"Tell me," Sophie demanded.

"Open the door and find out."

"What?" Sophie paused, her mouth stretching into a wide grin. "You're here?"

"Come and find out," Evie repeated.

Without wasting another second, Sophie raced to the front door and flung it open. Sure enough, on the other side of the doorway, Evie was waiting with a large suitcase at her feet. Sophie hugged her tightly, getting a faceful of coffee-brown hair.

"I can't believe you're here."

Evie hugged back even tighter. Five-foot-three, with a curvy frame and breasts that were disproportionately large, Evie was made for hugging. Well, hugging, cuddling, and a wide variety of sexual activities. Simply looking at her was enough to make most men fall madly in lust. Sophie shot down a pang of envy before it could surface.

"What's the occasion?" Sophie asked when Evie finally let her go.

Evie's eyes opened wide, and she blinked innocently. "Since when do I need an occasion to visit my best friend?"

"Evie," Sophie said, cajoling. There was always an occasion with Evie. She had good intentions, but some scheme was always in the works, and disaster often followed.

"Fine." Evie laughed easily. "My work contract finished, and I'm between jobs. But I've got something else lined up. I just need a place to stay for a few days. Is that cool?"

Evie went through several jobs each year. The longest she had ever stayed anywhere was eight months. She had been a dairy farmer, a cashier, a waitress, a receptionist, a gardener, a nanny, and had even taken a course in graphic design. Sophie used to try to keep track of Evie's work but had long since given up.

"When are you leaving and where are you going?" she asked, genuinely interested. It must be fascinating to experience so many different workplaces and cultures. It just wasn't for Sophie. She had her mother to take care of. Speaking of… "Evie, I really need to get Mum some dinner. Do you mind coming with me? You can dump your stuff in the spare room."

Evie's expression softened. "How is Antonia?"

"The same as always. Sometimes I think she's making progress, but then…" Her throat clogged.

Evie understood. "She shuts down, or her symptoms get worse. I'm sorry, Soph. Are you sure it's not too much of a hassle if I stay?"

Sophie nodded firmly. "It'll be great to have company."

Although what she was going to do when her handsome male company turned up was a mystery.

Cooper and Evie knew each other. They had grown up together, just as Sophie and Cooper had. In fact, until a couple of days ago, she would have considered that Evie knew him better than she did. Cooper and Evie were both so free-spirited, but Sophie had the upper hand now. Unfortunately, Evie had lips like a well-oiled door: they couldn't help opening. If Cooper turned up, it wouldn't be long before Aria knew everything.

Sophie led Evie to the Big House, discreetly writing out a text to Cooper, explaining that he wouldn't be able to come over for a few nights. How disappointing.

"So, about your work?"

"I've been calving at a dairy farm. The season is over, so

I've found work at Penelope's Café in Dunedin. I start on Tuesday."

"Tuesday?" Sophie asked. "That's such a weird day to start working."

"I know," Evie agreed. "But Monday is their day off."

When they arrived at the Big House, Antonia's gaze flickered to Evie. She didn't say anything despite Evie's perky greeting. Sophie helped Antonia from the couch back to her bed, then started to spoon out some soup for her, but Antonia didn't respond. Instead, she let the soup dribble down her chin.

Sophie wasn't sure whether her mother's muscles were failing, or she simply couldn't bear being fed in front of a young, lively woman.

Sophie sighed. "Please, Mum. Cooperate with me. You have to eat something."

But her mother remained silent. Antonia could be damned stubborn, and Sophie knew a lost battle when she saw one. The soup went back into the fridge.

CHAPTER 6

Sophie and Evie got Chinese takeout. In between mouthfuls of sweet and sour pork and fried noodles, Evie regaled Sophie with stories of her travels, and in return Sophie told her about Aria's whirlwind romance.

"So, this Eli is a looker?" Evie asked.

"Of epic proportions," Sophie confirmed. Thinking of good-looking guys made her think of Cooper. Eli might be refined, but Cooper was raw, and it made him so much more attractive. "But not the sexiest man I've ever met."

Evie groaned and tugged at her hair in frustration. "Not Evan again? You have to get over that one, Soph. He's nice to look at, but he's a bad guy."

Startled, Sophie couldn't help laughing. "You're so behind. I dumped his ass like a week ago."

"For real?"

"Yeah. And really, Evie, get off your high horse. Look at the relationships you've been in. Richard was high twenty-four-seven, Tim stared at everyone, and let us not forget Marie."

Evie narrowed her eyes. "Marie was beautiful."

"She was a psycho."

"Touché."

A gorgeous, leggy blonde with a perfect pink pout, Marie had seemed sweet at first. Then she'd become paranoid about Evie's relationships with others. Men and women, friends, acquaintances. She had tried to shut Evie off from other people, bit by bit. Luckily, Evie was smarter than people gave her credit for and had seen right through her. It was a close call.

Both women shivered.

"We should go out tonight," Evie said. "Visit a few bars, flirt up a storm. Maybe take someone home." She waggled her eyebrows suggestively. "You're free to have a wild fling now."

Sophie's eyes slid away from Evie's. Was she free? She'd never asked if she and Cooper were having an open fling or an exclusive one. Did exclusive flings exist? *Don't be silly,* she chided herself. *Of course they don't.* She was free to flirt with, and kiss, any man she wanted.

"Okay," Sophie agreed.

Evie's eyes brightened. Then her entire countenance perked up. "This is going to be just like old times."

Sophie looked at the ceiling. They'd engaged in more than their fair share of reckless behavior back in the day. "God, I hope not."

FOR THE SECOND time in less than a week, Sophie let one of her friends dress her. If she didn't put a stop to this silliness before long, she'd begin to feel like a Barbie doll. Then again, no Barbie had ever been short and ginger.

Still, she had to admit that she liked what Evie had done with her. The black dress she'd squeezed into shimmered with thousands of sequins and pinched inwards at the waist while emphasizing her rounded butt. A push-up bra did wonderful things for her chest. The contrast between the black dress and her hair was startling, but in a good way. Her complexion, on the other hand... Too pale. Oh, well. Some things never changed.

"You look fabulous," Evie declared, satisfied with her work.

"You look better," Sophie replied truthfully. With her creamy brown skin, silky hair and lush curves, Evie would always be the most desirable girl in any room. Her redeeming quality was that she didn't realize it.

It was dark when they arrived at Davy's bar. The music was throbbing so strongly, the windows rattled every few beats.

"Are we really going to this place again?" Evie asked distastefully.

"Davy's is the best!" Sophie exclaimed. "We always come here."

"Exactly. Been here, done that. Can't we go somewhere else?"

"Nope."

"I hate you."

"Love you, too."

They wriggled into the mass of writhing bodies, mostly tourists rather than locals, and moved in time with the bass-dominated club music. Evie latched on to a guy immediately. Sophie kept her distance, preferring to dance alone and people-watch.

The hours passed quickly in a blur of alcohol and dancing. Evie moved on to another guy and then *moved onto* him in a more literal sense. Sophie had to avert her eyes. Then a pair of hands landed on her waist, and she spun around to face an overly tanned guy several years her junior.

"No, thanks!" she shouted above the music, then extricated herself and crossed the room to sit at the bar.

"Not interested in a boy toy?" Davy asked as he refilled

her glass. She had to lean forward to understand his Irish brogue in the noisy bar.

"Not tonight," she replied.

"Are you seein' someone?"

She hesitated.

"You are!" he hooted. "Who?"

She shook her head, declining to comment.

"Go, Soph." His grin was wicked. "It's about damn time. What about Evan?"

"To hell with Evan."

"That's my girl."

Sophie smiled and wondered why she had never considered dating Davy. He was attractive, though not in a conventional way. His red hair and freckles were adorable as opposed to sexy, but he had big hands and muscular arms, which were displayed to great advantage in rolled-up shirtsleeves.

Davy groaned, and she turned to see what he was looking at. In the corner, Evie was hooking up with some guy Sophie had never met before—and it was Sophie's guess that Evie hadn't either.

"What is she doing?" he demanded. "She can't do that in my bar!"

"I've seen people do worse," Sophie said, watching as Evie broke away.

"The girl needs to learn some self-respect."

Davy stepped out from behind the counter and confronted the amorous duo. Sophie couldn't hear the words they exchanged, but Evie's gestures grew angry, then she took the unfamiliar man by the hand and left the bar.

"Now you've done it," she muttered, following Evie out the door. "Evie!" she called, and Evie stopped and waited for her to catch up. Sophie pressed a key into her palm. "Call a taxi and go home." Directing a meaningful glance at the mystery man, she added, "Alone."

"But I don't want to go home," Evie giggled. "I'm having so much fun with Joseph."

"Go home," Sophie repeated.

"Oh, all right." Evie heaved a sigh. "But you're being a killjoy. Where are you going?"

Sophie bit her lip and tried to think of a convincing lie. She failed. "I'm going to visit my lover."

Evie giggled again, her foiled romance forgotten. "Good one, Soph. Your lover. You have a good time now."

Sophie watched her get in a taxi alone. Then she started a long walk. She was looking forward to seeing Cooper again, and she was going to show him exactly how much.

Cooper felt quite put out by the text he'd received from Sophie earlier in the day. After listening to her voice message, which was filled with promise, he'd been excited to see her again. Then she'd disappointed him with six blunt words.

Can't see you tonight. Evie's here.

"Damnit," he muttered as he lay in bed, lonely and unsatisfied. He closed his eyes and pictured Sophie the way she had been last night. Hair mussed, cheeks flushed, eyes sparkling with desire. *Bad idea, mate.* Now he was burning with want for her all over again. Why did he have so much pent-up lust for one woman? It confused him.

Eyes open, he stared at the ceiling. And then, there she was. As if he had summoned her, she appeared above him in a glittering dress. It made no sense, but he wasn't going to argue.

"Sophie," he breathed. "What are you doing here?"

"I'm here to see you," she replied. "Don't go to sleep yet. There are so many other things we could do together."

He laughed tightly. "Believe me, sweetheart, sleep is the last thing on my mind."

"I'm glad to hear that," she said. Then she licked her lips.

The delicate movement sent a bolt of desire directly to Cooper's groin, bypassing his brain. He pitched a tent in the sheet.

Her eyes tracked over him, and she grinned smugly. "You're happy to see me."

"Pretty girl turns up in my room late at night? Of course I'm happy." He didn't try to disguise the need in his voice. In his experience, women liked to feel powerful. They did wonderful things to him when he made them feel powerful. "But what about Evie?"

"Evie is probably passed out on my couch by now."

"Drunk?"

"Yeah, but not so much that she needs me."

As much as he didn't want to think about Evie's wellbeing when he could be touching Sophie, he resisted the urge to reach for her. "You sure she'll be okay?"

"She'll be fine, Coop. Evie always bounces back. Now, forget about her and think about us." As she spoke, she turned and sat on the edge of the bed, her back towards him. "Unzip me."

He sat, swung his legs off the side of the bed, and did as he was told. The dress was high-necked but short, the zip running from neck to bottom. Cooper undid it an inch at a time, pressing kisses to her skin as it was revealed bit by bit. He hadn't expected to have her tonight, but now that he did, he was going to take his damn time.

"Coop," she groaned in frustration. "It should have been a two-second job."

Her impatience made him smile. "Relax, sweetheart. There's no need to hurry."

"I want you, now."

"I want you too. All night long."

She didn't argue further, but he knew better than to assume he'd won. Inhaling deeply, he breathed in the scent of her. Perfume, sweat, and something else. Something he couldn't put his finger on. Finally, the dress gaped open and she allowed it to slide off and pool at her feet.

"Better?" he asked.

"I will be as soon as you touch me," she replied. Her breasts were popping out the top of a bra, and her panties were no more than a tiny scrap of silk.

He swallowed. "God, you're beautiful." Her cheeks flushed and she smiled, but there was something unusual about her smile, something a little bit shy, as if she didn't believe him. Somehow, it was imperative that she believe him. "Come here," he ordered.

"Yes, sir," she replied, stepping closer.

Cooper cupped her breasts in his hands, his palms supporting them while his fingers brushed the soft skin exposed above the edge of the bra. "These are perfect," he said.

He lowered his head to kiss each breast, reaching around to undo the clasps so she was freed of the bra. She filled his hands perfectly, and her pink nipples made him salivate.

"They're small," she murmured, and the flush extended down her neck onto the breasts he wanted to worship.

"They're exactly the right size," he said. "Don't ever say they're not perfect."

She looked like she might argue, but she stopped when he set his mouth over her pale skin, his tongue stroking her nipple, drawing it deeper into his mouth. She whimpered, and he turned his attention to her other breast, lips curling triumphantly as she gasped.

"Oh, Coop," she whispered. "Please, I need you."

"Not yet."

Denying himself was painful, but he'd seen the doubt in her eyes. She had to know how much he wanted her. For

God's sake, he was here with her despite her friendship with his sister. If he was treading in dangerous territory, it was damn well going to be worth their while. He banded his hands around her arms and swung her onto the bed with him. All she was wearing now was that scrap of silk. It had to go.

Cooper met Sophie's eyes and saw the heat in them. She was burning for him as much as he was burning for her. With flushed skin and disheveled hair, she looked wanton. Soft and womanly.

She rose on her elbows and frowned at him. "What are you...?"

"Lie down," he said.

"You're awfully bossy tonight," she replied, but she did as she was told.

Cooper crawled down the bed and studied the insides of her thighs, which were toned from running but smooth beneath his fingers as he stroked from her knee to just beneath her center. His lips followed his fingers, and she sighed his name as he stopped at the juncture of her thighs.

"Say you're beautiful," he ordered.

"Coop, please don't stop."

"Say it."

"Will it make you keep going?"

"Say it, Sophie." The words were a growl.

"I'm beautiful."

He rewarded her with his mouth on her core. Immediately, her hips bucked off the bed, and her breathing became labored. Cooper teased her with his tongue and fingers until he didn't think he could stand it anymore. She cried out in protest as he pulled away.

"I *have* to have you," he said. "Now."

"Yes," she agreed, breathless. "Yes, Coop. I need you inside me."

The words inflamed him. He sheathed himself deftly and thrust inside her. It was heaven.

"You're so ready for me," he groaned.

Sophie's eyes flickered shut as he began to move. They rocked slowly together at first, the languorous strokes stoking the desire within both of them. Their bodies slid over each other, limbs tangling together until they were intertwined. Every thrust drew a gasp from Sophie. She was speaking softly, quickly, but he couldn't make out the words.

It was so good. Being with her felt so good.

His thrusts became jerky and urgent; he didn't think he could hold on for much longer.

"Come, Soph," he said. "Come for me, baby."

Please don't let me unman myself. Not with her. He reached between them and thumbed her clit. A cry tore from her throat, and she convulsed around him. *Oh, thank God.* He slammed into her once, twice, then he was coming too, shaking so violently with the force of it that he had to grip the sheets to stop from grabbing her too hard and hurting her.

Eventually, the tremors stopped, and he opened his eyes to look deep into hers. They were blue, he realized. He had never paid attention before. He didn't know how he hadn't, when they were so deeply blue that he felt as if he could dive into them. Now they were sparkling up at him. Looking at him as if he had just brought her the most earth-shattering pleasure of her life. Which he had. He hoped.

THEY DIDN'T SPEAK. They just lay together, Cooper's large, muscular body covering Sophie's. She felt cherished, protected. She knew she ought not to feel that way, as it could only lead to heartbreak, but right now, in this moment, she enjoyed it and ignored the consequences. After all, she'd just had life-altering sex. Surely that had earned her a few moments' reprieve from the real world.

When Cooper rolled off and flopped onto his back next to her, she felt the loss.

"Every time I do that with you, it gets better," he said.

"So you should definitely keep doing it," she replied. "Just think what it'll be like in a couple of weeks."

He chuckled, and the sound made her heart flutter. "Amazing."

She smiled and resisted the urge to snuggle him. *No strings and no attachments,* she reminded herself. If she cuddled, it would make him uncomfortable and screw with her inner peace. Sophie had always had a masochistic streak, but it wasn't intentional. She avoided pain where she could.

Sneaking a glance at Cooper, with his unshaven chin and shaggy blond hair, his strong jaw and stronger body, she ached just to look at him, he was so handsome. Sophie could never be with someone so attractive and certain of his own appeal. Not permanently. It would end the same way her relationship with Evan had: in disaster. Still, she couldn't resist exploring his torso with her hands. It was tight, even when he was relaxed. Every muscle pronounced, shifting beneath his bronzed skin. He was built like a god. But he was marked, too. The signs of a dangerous life decorated his body: thin white scars scattered across his chest, legs and arms. The brutal scar crossing his stomach drew her attention. She ran a finger along the crease of it, and he shivered.

She snatched her hand away. "I'm sorry. Did that hurt?"

"No. It's just sensitive."

Turning to him, she noticed for the first time that his expression was serious. "What is it?" she asked.

"Nothing." He shook his head, but his eyes were clouded.

Curiosity overcame any concern she'd felt over his odd mood. "How did you get that scar?"

"It's a long story."

Sophie wrapped her arms around herself as the sweat began to cool on her skin. "I've got time."

He moved away from her. "It's a war story. You don't really want to hear it."

"Of course I do. The wound must have been painful."

"It was," he confirmed. "But it's old news. Barely even bothers me anymore."

He wouldn't meet her eyes, so perhaps she'd overstepped. They'd never agreed to share confidences, and he clearly didn't like her prying into his past.

"You should go home," he said, standing so that he was looking down on her.

"Did I do something wrong?" she asked in a small voice. How had they gone from fantastic sex to eviction in only a few minutes?

"No." Cooper ran a hand through his hair and sighed. He met her gaze, his expression rueful. "You were great."

"Then, why are you trying to get rid of me?" She was hurt, and she knew it showed. Damn it. She'd never been good at concealing her emotions.

Cooper's expression softened and he took her hand, then pulled her so she was standing close to him. All that separated them was a few millimeters of air—and their secrets.

"I don't sleep with women," Cooper replied, and she felt the sting of being lumped in with his other women again. But then, she'd asked for this. She'd wanted a fling with a notorious playboy. She wouldn't roll over easily, like one of his other women, though. There was more than one way to play this game.

Sophie leaned toward him, lifting her lips to his ear. "Who said anything about sleeping?"

CHAPTER 7

It was the best Monday morning Sophie could remember. Not that she particularly thought of Mondays, or of any other day, for that matter. But on this particular Monday, she woke early with a large male arm draped over her waist. She snuggled back against a solid chest, wriggling her bum. Cooper made a sound of surprise deep in his throat, but then he warmed to having her there. A lot. She might even go as far as to say he melted her with his heat.

Once they'd cooled down, they set out on a run together, lifted weights when they returned home, then showered, the latter quickly devolving into a slippery fumble against the shower wall. Sophie loved every moment of it. It felt so right, so natural. Afterwards, she went home to help with Antonia's morning routine and dress for work.

Her high lasted all day, and her sales showed it. With two offers on the table, it was going to be a good payday. Maybe she'd be able to squirrel away some money for herself. With Antonia's care and the bills, she didn't often save money. She tried; she really did. But it was difficult being a single woman with a dependent mother.

When she arrived home that evening, Evie was lying sprawled on the sofa, snoring softly. Sophie rolled her eyes. From years of experience, she knew Evie could sleep through a bulldozer driving through the front door. She prepared rice and vegetables for dinner, shared a bowl with Antonia, then shook Evie awake.

"Hey, babe," she said. "Wake up."

"Soph?" Evie asked, rubbing her eyes. "What time is it?"

Sophie glanced at her watch. "Seven o'clock, give or take."

"Oh, shit." Evie lurched upright. "I should be gone already. I need to be in Dunedin tonight."

"It's not too late," Sophie assured her. "The InterCity bus passes through at eight-thirty."

"Thank God." Evie sank to the sofa again and laughed. "Crisis averted."

Sophie offered her a bowl of dinner. "I thought you might want to eat before you leave."

"Thanks." Evie took the bowl and dug in. "Mm, it's good."

"It's rice. Hard to mess it up."

Evie rolled her eyes. "Learn to take a compliment. Hey, where did you go last night?"

Feeling a flush creep over her cheeks, Sophie turned away. "What do you mean?"

"You weren't here when I woke up. Where were you?"

In Cooper Simons' bed. Rubbing against his fabulous body. Her blush deepened. "I went for a run." Technically, it was the truth.

Evie paused, studying Sophie's cheeks. It was unlike Sophie to lie, and Evie knew it, but those red cheeks told tales. "You were with a man."

Sophie sighed. "It wouldn't be the first time."

"Was it Evan?"

"Please," Sophie scoffed. "Have some faith in me." Evie just looked at her. "No," she said, a bit annoyed. "It wasn't."

"Then, who?"

"A man. It doesn't really matter. It's just a casual thing." She crossed her fingers that her blasé attitude would convince Evie, even though she didn't buy it herself.

Evie smiled, accepting the half-truth. "You haven't seen anyone else since you started seeing Evan. I'm happy for you. Is he good?"

Sophie closed her eyes, remembering the way Cooper's skin had felt against hers, the way they fit together so seamlessly. "Mind-blowing," she replied honestly. "The best of my life."

"That's great. But remember the number one rule."

"*Keep it casual,*" Sophie quoted. "I will. It's just..." She sighed. "We're so good together. Makes it easy to think it means more."

"But it doesn't," Evie reminded her. "To men, sex doesn't have to mean anything."

Evie sounded surprisingly bitter for an open-minded woman. It had always seemed to Sophie that her friend preferred not to have any entanglements. But maybe she'd done her a disservice by thinking that. Maybe someone had hurt her.

"Men use women, Soph," Evie said, tilting her chin up. "But there's no harm in using them back."

Sophie wasn't comfortable with the direction of the conversation and stayed silent.

Evie finished her bowl of rice. "We should go. I want to see Aria's baby bump before I leave."

The implication hung heavy in the air between them: Evie didn't know when she'd next be in Itirangi. She never did.

"It's not much of a bump at the moment," Sophie told her.

"Then I'll be the weird person stroking a flat belly." Evie grinned. "That's all good."

. . .

THE SUN HAD ALREADY SUNK low outside when they headed for Aria's place. The days were becoming cooler and the nights, longer. The leaves on the oak trees lining the road were the color of sunset, and many littered the footpath.

"I *hate* this town," Evie said vehemently, watching it pass by the car window.

Sophie frowned. Part of her agreed, but another part of her truly loved her home. "It's a beautiful town."

"I feel like there's no room for me to breathe," Evie explained. "It chokes me. Can't you feel it? Like it's strangling the life from me. Why do you stay here?"

"Because of my mother," Sophie replied sharply. "I can't leave."

"I'm sorry. I shouldn't have said—"

"Forget about it."

They arrived at Aria's house, and Sophie noticed a car parked in the drive: a shiny black Jaguar.

"Nice ride." Evie's voice was full of admiration. "The elusive Mr. Lockwood's?"

Sophie nodded as they got out of the car, but she wasn't sure Evie saw the gesture.

Light was emanating from the kitchen window. Sophie knocked on the front door, but no one replied. Evie moved to open it.

"Wait." Sophie shot out a hand to stop her. "Just for a moment."

Evie shook her off impatiently. "Why? It's Aria. She's like family."

"Did you ever see your mum naked?" Sophie asked.

Evie screwed up her nose. "Aw, man. I don't even want to think about it."

"Unless you want to see Aria naked, give them a moment."

"But she's pregnant," Evie protested.

Sophie laughed. "So? She's pregnant, not dead. When you see Eli, you'll understand."

They waited in silence for a couple of minutes that seemed to drag on for much longer.

"Do you think they're...?" Evie asked.

Sophie shook her head. "No. They heard us."

Finally, the door opened, and Aria hurried out and flung her arms around Evie. "I'm so glad to see you!" she said. Her cheeks were flushed, her hair and clothing disheveled. "Come in."

Eli was waiting in the kitchen. "Hi, Sophie," he said, his smile smug and satisfied. "And you must be Evie."

"The famous Elijah Lockwood," Evie said, angling her head to appraise him. "I get it now."

He winked at her. "I do, too."

Aria smiled broadly, completely unconcerned by the light flirtation, secure in Eli's love. She'd never looked more beautiful. With a baby in her belly and her man on her arm, Aria was practically glowing, and Sophie felt a pang of bittersweet jealousy. Aria deserved happiness. God knew she was a better person than Sophie, but still, Sophie couldn't help wishing she had some of that happiness for herself.

Evie caught sight of the rock on Aria's finger and gushed over it. "When's the big day?"

"September," Eli replied.

"That's only a few months away," Evie said, shocked. "That's hardly any time to plan a wedding."

"We don't care," Aria replied. "We just want to be married. It will only be a small wedding at a venue near the lake."

"I'm so happy for you," Sophie said. And she was.

Dammit, she was.

Cooper scooped a generous portion of dip onto his plate, then grabbed a handful of chips and a beer before striding into the lounge and flopping onto the couch. It was a familiar situation: him, Justin, beers and rugby at Justin's house on the outskirts of Itirangi, backing onto a nature reserve. Tonight, the New Zealand All Blacks were playing the South African Springboks. The All Blacks were expected to win; they usually did. But the Springboks were strong adversaries. It could be a close game. On screen, the teams were warming up.

"D'you get me a beer?" Justin asked.

"Get your own," Cooper replied, then propped his feet on the coffee table after Justin had left the room, moving a vase out of the way with his toe.

"Feet down," Justin ordered as soon as he returned.

"Really, mate?" Cooper asked in exasperation. "They're not doing any harm."

Fidgeting with the beer cap, Justin sighed heavily. "Just get them down. Emily doesn't like feet on furniture."

Emily was messing with their traditions. But, no surprise there. Women did that when you allowed them into your heart and your home. Not that Cooper was particularly experienced on that front. None of his relationships ever lasted longer than two months.

"You're wrapped around her little finger," he muttered, lifting his feet off the table. "There are flowers on your coffee table, for God's sake."

Justin sculled his beer and slammed the can down. "I like having her in my life. I'm not ashamed of that. If I have to put up with a few bouquets of flowers around the house, I can handle it."

Cooper raised an eyebrow. "You can handle flowers? Really? What about that breakdown you had over the pink fluffy thing in your bathroom?"

Justin shrugged. "Not a big deal. I've got my priorities straight. Emily makes me happy. Deal with it."

Cooper wondered what had happened to his gruff, unemotional brother. How had he fallen for a florist who believed the world was rainbows and unicorns? Few men could resist Emily's charming blend of prettiness and sweetness, but he'd have thought his brother was one of the number who could. But good for Justin. He'd had a rough time with women. The least Cooper could do was be supportive.

"I'm glad you've got Emily," he said, and it was true. This version of Justin—relatively chipper—was unfamiliar, but pleasant.

"I wish you'd settle for one girl," Justin remarked.

A cold finger wiggled down Cooper's spine. "Where did that come from?"

"I think it'd be good for you."

The rugby players began singing the national anthem. Cooper watched them, ignoring his holier-than-thou brother. He and Aria were as bad as each other, wanting everyone to settle into domestic bliss. "You don't know what would be good for me."

Justin eyed him thoughtfully. "Come to think of it, I haven't seen you with any girls lately."

"Is that so unusual?"

"Yes," Justin replied decisively. "You typically have a waiting period of a couple of days between women. You finished with Gemma several days ago. Since then, I haven't received any texts bragging about the new hottie in your life. What gives?"

"I told you I was taking a break from women," Cooper said, smothering any feeling of guilt over his arrangement with Sophie.

He and Sophie had done a lot of things together, things that made him hard just remembering them, but they certainly weren't taking a break. He'd had morning sex for the first time, and it had been wonderful. He hadn't spent the night with a woman since he'd returned, but Sophie was different. He didn't know how, only that she was.

"I don't think you're capable of taking a break from women," Justin said. "So, who is she? The woman you're keeping a secret."

Cooper fought to keep his cool. "There's no woman."

"Yeah, right."

"There's no girl," Cooper snapped.

Justin's eyes widened, but he didn't comment. Silence was a more effective interrogation technique.

"If there was a girl, I'd tell you." The lie burned Cooper's tongue. He tried again. "Why would I keep it secret?"

"Perhaps she's much younger, or much older, or a guy."

Coop appreciated the attempt at humor. "I'm not gay," he said. "I can appreciate a nice set of biceps as much as the next guy, but I definitely like women." Then the game started, and Cooper helped himself to another chip with dip and washed it down with a swig of beer. "Tell you what. If I meet a special woman, I'll let you know."

Justin nodded, accepting the olive branch. "Cheers."

After that, their conversation centered on the game. The All Blacks won, as expected, but Cooper was too distracted to care. All night, he pondered whether he was really as much of a womanizer as his brother claimed. He thought maybe he was, and that bothered him.

CHAPTER 8

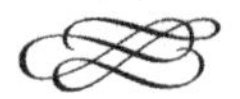

Cooper woke from his nightmare with sweaty palms and adrenaline pounding through his body. His fists clenched the sheets. It had been especially bad this time, every memory more vivid, the taste of blood in his mouth, the bite of shrapnel in his skin. No way in hell could he sleep again after that. Not tonight.

He sat up and tossed the sheet off, wishing for someone to talk to, someone who could understand. If only Ben were still alive. Ben had always known what to say. But he wasn't, and Cooper had to deal with that.

Balling up the top sheet, he grimaced. Drenched again. He rubbed his eyes and glanced at the clock. 2 a.m. Just great. With a heavy sigh, he left the bed and turned the shower on, then waited until the water was scalding hot before he stepped under it. Closing his eyes, he let the water rinse the sweat off his body, which took the sharp edge off the visions in his head, leaving them blurred and distorted. He opened his eyes. The image of Ben faded until it was nothing more than a hazy reflection in the glass.

His brain loved to torture him this way, reminding him of

what he'd lost. Or, more accurately, of what he hadn't been strong enough to save.

Cooper turned away from the glass, stepped out of the water, and buried his face in a towel as he dripped freely on the bathroom floor. After taking a few deep breaths to regain control, he toweled off briskly and stared himself in the eye in the mirror above the vanity.

"Pull yourself together, man."

The face that looked back at him could have been a stranger's. Damn. The empty space in his chest felt suffocating. He smashed his fist down on the vanity, pleased by the jolt of pain that ricocheted up his arm to his elbow. It grounded him, gave him something in the real world to hold on to. He tore away, strode back to the bedroom, and pulled on a pair of jeans and a sleeveless shirt.

Outside, the cold air bit into his warm skin, but he ignored it as he locked the house and climbed behind the wheel of his car. He hadn't made a conscious decision to leave, so he found himself ready to go but with no destination in mind. For a moment, he contemplated parking outside Trisha and Madison's house, just to reassure himself they were safe, but decided against it. He hadn't descended that far into madness yet.

Sophie.

She was his for another week and a half. Although it was late, she might be prepared to open her door for him if he was charming enough—and Cooper knew how to be charming. Decision made, he sped to her place, the scenery flying past the windows of the car. In short order, he stood on her doorstep.

After freezing for several minutes with no response to his knocks, he was beginning to feel stupid when the door swung open and Sophie blinked up at him sleepily. She shivered when the cool air hit her and drew her lumpy bathrobe more tightly around herself.

"Coop?" she asked, a slight furrow forming between her eyebrows. "What are you doing here?"

"I... I..." he stammered, struck mute by the sight of her. He'd been prepared for Sophie the seductress, and he could have handled that woman. He didn't know what to do with the sleepy, adorable version of Sophie. Sometimes he forgot how small she was, not even reaching his shoulder. He could easily pick her up with one arm. So petite. Breakable.

Memories of carnage and destruction flashed through his mind. A woman like Sophie had no place in a world where men like him killed and burned things to the ground.

"Hey." She must have glimpsed his turmoil, because she stepped down onto the doorstep, wrapped her arms around his waist, and squeezed tightly. "It's okay. I'm glad you're here."

Cooper returned the embrace and rested his cheek on the top of her head, breathing in the strawberry scent of her. It felt right, holding her like this. Like she had been made for him.

She drew back, tilting her head to meet his eyes. "Come in."

He shouldn't. Just being here broke all of his rules, but she seemed to know what he needed, and for once he was going to let someone else take the reins.

Winding his fingers through hers, he smiled hesitantly. She smiled back, stretched onto her tiptoes and pressed a kiss to his lips. The touch was soft and fleeting, but it zinged through Cooper and shook him to the core. What was she doing to him? He'd never felt so unsettled, and all because of a pint-sized woman.

Sophie led him into the bedroom. Unlike the last time he'd been here, the place was a mess. Clothes lay in piles on the floor, makeup was stacked haphazardly on the cupboard, and a set of free weights had been dumped in the corner with a yoga mat, yet another sign that he'd caught her off-guard.

Somehow, though, the mess relaxed him, which was surprising for a military man who kept a minimalistic house. He could picture Sophie living in this room. It felt like a home.

She retrieved a massive purple pillow from the floor and put it at the head of the bed, shucked the dressing gown to reveal a tiny pair of pajamas, and slipped under the duvet.

"You gonna join me?" she asked.

With a jolt, he realized she wanted him to take the spot next to her. He dithered, so far out of his comfort zone it was ridiculous.

"You can stand there like a doofus if you want, but it's warmer in here."

Hell, why not? If he was going to break the rules, he might as well do it properly. He unzipped his jeans, added them to a pile on the floor, and scooted into the bed, sliding an arm around her.

"Do you wanna talk about it?" she asked.

"No." He wouldn't be able to stand seeing the shock in her eyes. Or worse, the pity.

"Okay," she said simply, then rested her head on his shoulder and closed her eyes. "Do you mind getting the light?"

Glancing around, he noticed a switch on the wall to his right and flicked it, plunging them into darkness. Sophie hummed contentedly and snuggled closer, and Cooper's mind spun, trying to catch up. He couldn't figure out how he'd ended up here. All he'd wanted was a quick screw to take his mind off things. Instead, he'd morphed into a speechless zombie and let her coddle him. And the worst part was, he liked it. He liked listening to Sophie's soft breaths becoming regular as she dropped off to sleep. Liked feeling the warm length of her next to him. Most of all, he liked that after he finally fell asleep himself, he didn't dream.

~

SOPHIE WOKE to the buzz of her vibrating alarm on the bedside table. Groaning, she switched it off and eased out of bed, careful not to wake Cooper, who was snoozing next to her.

He'd barely spoken after he'd turned up on her doorstep in the middle of the night. God knew what demons had driven him here, but she'd known not to press him for fear of making him shut down completely. Still, she was pleased he'd found some measure of peace during the night—and he must have, or he wouldn't have fallen asleep.

Years ago, climbing into Sophie's bed had been enough to ease Antonia's pain. Unfortunately, Antonia could no longer walk to Sophie's bed unassisted, much less climb in.

Yanking on her robe, Sophie grimaced, noticing the state of the room *and herself*. Oh, jeez. She'd opened the door wearing the ugliest thing she owned and had let him into a room in worse condition than what most teenagers would tolerate. Then again, considering the way he'd stared at her blankly, he might not have seen much of anything.

One could hope.

Sophie cooked a bowl of porridge—the morning air was too chilly for an uncooked breakfast—and trekked down the path to the Big House. A pile of fresh laundry was folded on the sofa, evidence the nurse had visited.

Knocking on the bedroom door, Sophie called, "Mum? You up?"

No response. She pushed the door open a crack and peered in to see Antonia rolling over in bed. Good, she was awake. Shoving the door wide open, Sophie breezed into the room, whipped the curtains back and spun around to smile at her mother. "Good morning," she chirped. "How are you doing today?"

Antonia glared at her through half-closed eyes. "I *was* fine."

Cheeky. She must be in good spirits. Sophie perched on the edge of the bed, the bowl of porridge in her lap. "You going to work with me today, Mum?"

Antonia heaved a long-suffering sigh. "I suppose so. But it's so...lowering."

"I know." Sophie kissed her cheek. "I'm sorry. I wish I could make it better."

After helping her shift upright, Sophie propped a pillow against the head of the bed and laid the bowl on the bedding in front of her mother. Leaving the bowl where it was, Antonia scooped a spoonful of porridge and lifted it to her mouth, spilling a little down the front of her nightshirt. Sophie grabbed a tissue from her pocket and wiped the spill. They worked together until the bowl was empty, then Sophie turned the stereo on and moved the bowl from the bed. Trying to act casual despite her racing heart, she selected a romance novel from the bookshelf in the hall and handed it to her mum.

"I think you'll like this one," she said.

"Mm. Perhaps."

Antonia didn't so much as glance down at the cover, but Sophie's heart swelled. She hadn't immediately rejected the idea. That was an improvement. A slight one, but still, it gave Sophie some hope.

"Shall I read you a chapter to get started?"

"If you must."

Sophie read to her, introducing the hero and heroine but stopping as soon as she got to the juicy meet-cute. Hopefully, she'd piqued Antonia's interest enough for her to continue on her own. Sophie kissed her mum on the cheek and left to prepare for work, hoping against hope that Antonia would make the effort to read a chapter or two during the day. It wasn't healthy for a mind to be completely occupied with the past.

~

COOPER SHIFTED from his position behind the bookcase, his mind racing with questions. Sophie's mum was bedridden with some sort of illness. How had he not known that after he'd spent so much time with her over the last few days?

Because you're selfish. He was obsessed with his own problems. All the while, poor Sophie had been taking care of her mum. What was her name? Something unusual. Andrea? Anthea? *Antonia*. That was it. He wondered what was wrong with Antonia. Sophie had read to her like a parent to a child, except with raunchier material.

He'd felt like a pervert the whole damn time, watching them without announcing his presence, but he'd been so shocked, the wind had been knocked out of him. He'd never imagined Sophie had anything so serious going on in her life. It made him feel like the worst kind of criminal, making assumptions and taking advantage of a vulnerable woman.

Only... *She started it.*

The arrangement had been Sophie's idea to begin with, right down to the two-week expiry date. Had she set the time limit to stop him from getting close to her? Did she *want* to keep him out of her personal life? The thought made him unaccountably angry, especially after he'd come to her last night and exposed a facet of his damaged soul. She'd welcomed him into her bed without any questions. And once again, with her body tucked against his, he hadn't dreamed. Somehow, she eased the symptoms of his PTSD.

Cooper rubbed his eyes, frustrated. Sophie was a complicated woman, and for the first time he wondered if agreeing to her time limit had been a mistake. The more he saw of her, the more he wanted to see, and he worried that his feelings for her were no longer casual.

Taking a deep breath to steady himself, Cooper strode into the bedroom where Antonia was resting on the pillows, the book lying untouched on her lap.

"Hey, there," he said with false cheer. "How are you doing?"

"I'm okay," Antonia replied, her lips moving clumsily, as if speaking were unfamiliar. The words slurred together. Perhaps she'd had a stroke. "And you?"

"Good," he replied, leaning against the wall beside her bed. "I didn't realize you were sick. What is it?"

Her eyes shuttered as if she'd drawn the blinds. Her lips pursed, and she lifted her chin slightly but didn't reply.

"Is it treatable?" he asked, struck by the thought that she could be terminally ill.

After a moment, she said, "No."

"I'm so sorry." And he was. Poor Antonia. And poor Sophie. Why hadn't she mentioned her mother? Surely she knew he was an understanding guy. She'd been there for Cooper, and he'd like to return the favor if she'd give him a chance.

"It's not your fault," she said, looking down.

He felt like he wasn't seeing something here, but he couldn't put his finger on it. "I'm still sorry for you."

"Th-thank you." Her voice was rusty, like hinges on a gate that hadn't been opened in years. "Do..." She trailed off, took a breath and started again. "Do you..." This time, she squared her shoulders and made a visible effort to speak. "Love my daughter?"

Cooper chuckled. Of all the questions he might have expected, that one hadn't even made the list, but perhaps it should have. After all, what else would the mother of the woman he was seeing ask? But Cooper wouldn't know. He actively avoided mothers—other than his own, of course.

Although he loved women in general, his relationships never lasted for long, and he was afraid his girlfriends' mothers would see right through him. He didn't need any all-seeing, all-knowing older women realizing that his behavior was a result of PTSD and trying to fix him. He didn't need to be fixed.

"I don't love Sophie," he said honestly. "I care about her, but I don't love her."

Antonia nodded, deep in thought. "Could you?"

"Love her?" His eyebrows shot up. The question had surprised him. "She's a very lovable person, but I don't think I could love anyone. My heart's pretty ugly, Mrs. D. No one would want it, anyway."

His comments were intended to sound flippant, but instead they screamed of bitterness. Strange. He hadn't realized he cared about the state of his heart.

Antonia looked at him knowingly but didn't say anything. She'd run out of words. Cooper leaned over and kissed her cheek.

"Feel better," he said, then strolled out of the room, back towards Sophie's cottage, wondering how the hell he was going to get the truth out of her. He needed to know what was wrong with Antonia, and he wanted to pay Sophie back by being there for her the same way she'd been there for him.

CHAPTER 9

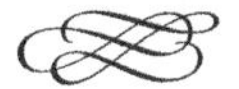

She'd gone.

A pot of coffee was brewing on the kitchen counter and she'd scrawled a note next to it that said, *Help yourself*, but there was no sign of Sophie. Had she seriously left without saying goodbye?

Cooper had avoided sleeping with a woman since he'd gotten back from Iran, but he'd broken his rule for her. Twice. It would have been nice if she'd stuck around and had breakfast with him, or at least acknowledged that it meant something for him to stay with her. He didn't want to be treated like any other lover, damn it. Turning to her when he was haunted by the nightmare of his past was momentous for him. *And I'd bloody well appreciate it if you recognized that.*

He poured a cup of coffee and gulped it down, then, before he could second-guess himself, tapped Sophie's number into his phone. It rang and rang with no answer. Her perky voice sounded over voicemail, and he hung up without leaving a message.

Shit, he was worse than some of the girls he'd dated, calling and hanging up. Changing tack, he called his sister.

"Hey, Ri," he said when she answered.

"Hi, Coop."

"You at work?"

Aria worked as a reporter for the local newspaper. It was through her work that she'd met her fiancée, Eli.

"Yeah," she said, "but if you give me a moment, I'll go somewhere quiet so we can talk."

"Thanks." He slurped more coffee and made himself comfortable on Sophie's raggedy sofa.

A few moments later, she asked, "What's up?"

Now that he had her undivided attention, he wasn't sure how to ask about Sophie or her mother without raising Aria's suspicions. How could he let on that he knew something was wrong without explaining what he'd been doing in Sophie's house when she wasn't around? If Aria knew he and Sophie were having sex, she'd never speak to him again.

He hadn't thought this through, and if he tried to act as if he just wanted to chat, she'd be on to him. She was the smart one in the family. He couldn't pull a fast one on her, but perhaps if he opted for a semi-truth, she'd be placated.

"There's a woman," he began hesitantly, uncertain how much to share. "She's different."

Aria chuckled. "She must be, if you're talking to me about her." She paused for a moment. "Her name isn't Bambi or Lola, is it?"

Cooper groaned. "Not you, too."

"What?" She sounded bemused.

"I'm capable of having a relationship with a classy woman."

"Of course you are." Her tone had turned serious. "You just haven't shown any particular interest in one woman in a long time. What gives?"

"Like I said, she's different."

"Can you be more specific?"

Not really, not without giving up his game. But perhaps he could talk about his feelings for Sophie rather than about her as a person. "You know I've had trouble sleeping for a few years now?"

"Yeah. Since you came back. I wish there was something I could do."

He winced, hating the pain in her voice. "She helps."

Aria didn't reply, and the moment dragged on. "Wow," she said finally. "That means something, Coop."

"I know. I sleep through the night when I'm with her, and there are no dreams. It's wonderful."

"But?"

He frowned. "What makes you think there's a 'but'?"

"With you and women, there always is. They're beautiful, *but* vindictive. Lovely, *but* insecure. Sweet, *but* there's no spark."

"Okay. Maybe the 'but' is that I'm just a fling to her. She keeps me at a distance, doesn't trust me with the things that matter. She's already given us an expiration date."

"Is that unusual for you? Aren't your women always temporary?"

While there was a certain irony in the situation, he didn't like being reminded of it. Had all the women he'd dated felt the way he was feeling now? As if there could be something real between them if he allowed it? It was a sobering thought.

"I guess," he muttered. "But how do I convince her to give us a chance?"

"What would a girl have to do for you to give *her* a chance?"

He pondered the question. If a girl ever tried to press him into a relationship, he cut her loose. It stood to reason that Sophie would do the same to him. She was fresh out of a bad relationship and looking to have a bit of fun, which was exactly what he'd promised her. He couldn't expect more simply because she cured his insomnia and kept his nightmares at bay, or because he loved the way she accepted him without question.

But he could be the perfect fling. Make her want to have him around for longer. Another day, which could turn into another week, and so on.

"Thanks, Ri," he said. "I think you've helped."

"Great! Are you going to tell me who she is?"

He shook his head, then remembered she couldn't see him. "Nope."

She sighed. "Thought as much. Good luck with your mystery girl."

"Thanks." He'd need it.

Sophie was buoyed by her first appointment of the day. She suspected she'd receive an offer from the prospective buyers by sunset. Her second and third appointments weren't as promising but could still come to something. By the time she met Aria for coffee at the bakehouse, things were looking good.

Her friend was sitting at their usual table next to the window overlooking Lake Itirangi. The sun was glittering off the turquoise water in such a way that the whole lake seemed to shimmer. Gorgeous. Sometimes, when she felt trapped, Sophie visited the bakehouse for one of their famous pies, looked out over the lake and reminded herself how lucky she was to live in this beautiful place. But this morning, she didn't need the reminder. She *felt* lucky.

Aria stood and hugged her. "Hey, Soph."

Sophie laughed delightedly. "You're glowing."

Aria beamed. "Eli says so, too."

"He's right," Sophie assured her. "You look great."

She'd always known that Aria would be the first of their friends to have children. Aria adored kids and had so much love to give to one of her own. Sophie knew the others had thought *she'd* be the first to get pregnant, but she was very careful whenever she slept with a man. She already had one dependent. She didn't need another.

"Thanks, sweetie," Aria said as they took their seats. "How are you today?"

"Can't complain," Sophie replied. "Anything new in your life?"

Aria grinned and leaned forward. Sophie got the feeling she was bursting to share some news. "You won't believe the phone call I got this morning."

"Who from?"

"Cooper." She laughed. "How the mighty have fallen. Get this: There's a new girl on the scene, and she's got him all stitched up."

All of a sudden, Sophie's heart stuttered and her breath hitched. Did Aria know? And more importantly, "What do you mean?"

"You know how there's a new woman every week with him."

"Yeah." Not that she wanted to think about him with any other woman.

"It seems like he's finally found someone he's interested in, but all she wants from him is sex." Aria chuckled. "Karma sucks."

Sophie forced herself to laugh, but even to her own ears, it sounded nervous. Was Aria talking about *her*? Was it possible that Cooper wanted more than a fling with her? No, it couldn't be. What a ridiculous thought. Why would he want her, when he'd dated dozens of hotties who made her look like a sack of potatoes? Sophie could be honest with herself. She might be in great physical shape, but she was short and flat-chested. Not exactly a notorious bachelor's ideal playmate.

"Yeah, right," she scoffed. "Coop isn't a one-woman man. I'll believe it when I see it."

"I didn't think you were such a cynic, Soph. I think he means it. Apparently, she helps his PTSD."

"What do you mean?" Sophie was beginning to feel like a broken record.

"The mystery woman," Aria said. "She stops his nightmares about the war."

Sophie ducked her head, listening carefully. Everyone knew Cooper had suffered a few episodes of PTSD after he returned, but she hadn't heard anything about it in years. "I didn't know that was still a problem for him."

Aria sighed. "Yeah. He stopped talking about it because he didn't want to make people uncomfortable, but the nightmares continued."

"How awful. That poor man."

Her heart ached for him. He'd probably been fleeing a nightmare when he'd turned up on her doorstep last night. She hadn't known what to make of him, standing there silently as if he was uncertain how he'd even arrived at her house. But he *had* gotten there, one way or another. When he was upset, he'd come to her, and knowing that caused a warm, fuzzy feeling to swell in her chest.

Uh-oh. Now she was in trouble.

This thing with Cooper was meant to be fun. Nothing more. If she started having *feelings*, she'd only get hurt, and she'd been hurt enough already.

"So, what are we going to do?"

Sophie glanced up. "Huh?"

Aria flicked a curl over her shoulder and rolled her eyes. "We've got to help Coop keep his mystery girl. But how?"

Great. This kept getting better and better. Not only did Aria know that Cooper was seeing someone, she wanted to interfere. At the moment, Aria had no idea whose bed Cooper was sharing, and it needed to stay that way. Unfortunately, Sophie had no idea how to put Aria off the scent. Hopefully, she wouldn't need to. Plenty of people had witnessed her and Cooper running together, but that was hardly damning. Except for their morning runs, they'd been discreet.

Sophie willed herself to relax. "Cooper's an adult. I'm sure he can work it out himself. He probably wouldn't like us sticking our noses in."

Aria stared at her. "He *called* me, Soph. In brother-speak, that's a gold-plated invitation to stick my nose in."

What the hell had been running through Cooper's thick skull when he called his sister? That was what Sophie would like to know. Surely he knew that if he gave an inch, she'd run a mile. Aria cared about her family and friends fiercely, which was one of the things Sophie loved about her, but she also had no boundaries when it came to their personal lives. When Aria saw a problem, she couldn't resist interfering. While her propensity for helping others had won her the love of her life, their journey hadn't been without its frustrations.

"What are you going to do?" Sophie asked, dreading the answer.

Aria shrugged. "I don't know yet. There's not much I *can* do until I know who she is."

"So, you'll let it go?"

"As if. I'll hound him until he tells me her name."

Sophie crossed her fingers that Cooper would keep his big mouth shut.

Of course, if she kept his mouth busy doing other things, he'd never get the chance to tell his sister anything.

Sophie began to smile. She had a plan.

Sophie kept Cooper occupied during his free time for the next two days. Doing so wasn't a hardship, since he seemed determined to make love to her every way he knew how—including a few positions she'd never tried before. He stopped extricating himself after they'd exhausted each other, instead curling his big body around hers and holding her until morning.

Sometimes, lying in his arms, she wondered about his nightmares and whether she really had cured them. Was it possible that simply being near her was enough to stop him from returning to a war zone while he slept? The thought both exhilarated and terrified her, making her feel special while simultaneously feeding her fear that she wouldn't be able to resist Cooper if he decided he wanted to extend their fling.

She already felt herself softening towards him. She *liked* him. But she couldn't afford to give him any more than the two weeks they'd agreed to. If she did, she risked losing her heart, and she wasn't prepared to do that.

So, on Friday, after their bodies had cooled, she untangled herself from him and dressed silently. After a moment, Cooper stirred.

"What are you doing?" he asked.

"Heading home," she replied. Surely it was obvious.

He came up on his elbows. "Why?"

Her heart hammered in her chest. She hadn't been prepared for that particular question. Hadn't their deal been 'no strings'? She shouldn't have to explain herself. "Because I'm tired."

It wasn't untrue. He might be used to getting by with minimal sleep, but his stamina had worn her out.

He frowned, the expression sitting oddly on his sleepy face. "Come back to bed."

She raised an eyebrow, surprised and a little annoyed by his commanding tone.

"We'll sleep," he promised. "That's all."

"I don't sleep very well with you in the bed." Now, *that* was a bare-faced lie. Being wrapped in his arms all night long was sublime.

"Oh." He had the decency to look chastened. "Sorry, I didn't realize."

"Don't worry about it," she said, guilt pricking her conscience. "But I want to sleep in my own bed tonight." He started to speak, and she held up a finger. "*Alone.*"

"Okay."

He didn't look the least bit sleepy anymore. Instead, he looked disappointed. Resigned, as if she were sentencing him to relive the worst moments of his life. She didn't want to put him through that, but she had to protect her heart first and foremost.

"If you change your mind, I'll be here," he said.

She nodded, meeting his eyes, which usually sparkled with mischief but now expressed such a depth of despair that she could barely stand to hold his gaze. Her knees weakened, and she longed to throw off her clothes and rejoin him in bed. What had he seen overseas to make the thought of dreaming bring him such sorrow? She couldn't even imagine.

Sophie bent and kissed him softly, then walked out the door.

Later, alone in her own bed, she didn't sleep a wink.

CHAPTER 10

Sophie finally dragged herself out of bed after playing games on her phone for an hour and dressed for a run. The sun was shining outside, so she opened a window in Antonia's bedroom and helped her get up, despite her objections. With the assistance of a walker, she guided Antonia outside, and they hobbled along the path to a comfortable chair by the garden, beneath the orange canopy of a pear tree. Sophie supported her mother while she descended into the seat, then fetched her a plate of crackers with tomato and avocado. This time, Antonia managed to eat without assistance.

Sophie sat on the ground and closed her eyes, absorbing the morning sun. She hoped with all her heart that Antonia was enjoying it, too. Sophie had read that Vitamin D from sunlight could help improve your mood, but with her mother's slack facial muscles, she couldn't form many expressions, and sometimes it was impossible to know how she felt because she didn't share much verbally, either.

"Are you happy here while I go for a run?" she asked her mum.

Antonia nodded, but as Sophie stood, her lips formed the

word 'Whitney'. Elated by the small victory, Sophie switched the stereo on. She fed Cletus a bowl of meat and a handful of treats, slipped her headphones into her ears and jogged down the street. The cold air burned her lungs, but her muscles warmed quickly, and the sun heated her back.

Passing through trees and across the golf course, she followed the footpath to the sports grounds, where a young family was passing a soccer ball around. The mum was slim and sporty, with brown hair that swung as she ran after the ball. Her daughter was petite and blonde. The dad was solidly built, with a golden mane that he shook out of his eyes frequently.

Hang on a moment... Sophie recognized that golden mane and those broad shoulders. If he came close, she'd bet that his eyes were blue, and his jaw was square. *Cooper.* But what was he doing here, playing with a pretty woman and her daughter as though they were a family?

Oh, shit.

Sophie's legs stopped moving and she stumbled forward, her knees skating across the gravel, stinging ferociously. Thankfully, she was far enough from the cozy family scene that no one noticed her fall. She picked herself up, then stepped back amongst the pine trees on the edge of the field, hoping they obscured her from view.

Her mind was racing. She'd thought *she* was the girl who'd cured Cooper's nightmares, but what if she was wrong? They'd never discussed exclusivity. He could have been dating the brunette on the soccer field while he was having a fling with Sophie. He'd never specifically said he was single when they slept together. She'd just assumed it.

She peered at the young girl. Surely not Cooper's daughter?

No. She shook her head. Of course not. A secret like that wouldn't last a week in Itirangi. But for Cooper to be so interested in the little girl's mum that he'd play daddy for the day, it must be serious.

The air gushed out of Sophie's lungs like she'd been sucker-punched. The truth was awful enough to strike bone-deep. If Cooper was dating that brunette, then Sophie herself was the other woman, the piece of ass on the side. She dropped to the ground again, pain shooting up her legs as she landed on her abused knees. She sucked in oxygen, her head swimming, her vision blurring. She would *not* cry, damn it. Not for a playboy she'd sworn she wouldn't get attached to. But how could he do this to her? He knew her past with Evan.

It was twisted. But then, men couldn't be trusted. They proved it again and again. She'd naively hoped for the best, regardless of all evidence to the contrary. Stupid, stupid girl.

When she could breathe again, Sophie jogged back the way she'd come. She couldn't handle confronting Cooper right now. In fact, she realized, she didn't have to confront him at all. This was a fling. No strings attached. If she wanted to end it early, that was her prerogative. She didn't owe him an explanation. She didn't owe any man anything. Screw them all.

SPENDING time with Trisha and Madison eased Cooper's mind. He'd woken from a nightmare and reached out for Sophie but found an empty bed instead. Strange how he'd become accustomed to having her there when they'd only spent a few nights together. It stood to reason, though, considering he hadn't shared a bed with anyone in years. He didn't understand why she'd left last night, but hopefully she was open to staying again tonight. After three blissful sleeps with no nightmares, having the bad dreams return had shaken him badly.

After lunch, Cooper flopped onto his couch and dialed Sophie's number. He'd need to leave for work soon, because today's bride, Emma, would begin to prepare at 2 p.m. for a casual evening wedding, his favorite type. The ceremony would be down by the lake, followed by a buffet dinner at the local pub, The Royal. Usually, he'd see the wedding as a chance to search for a replacement for Gemma, but this time he didn't need to. He had Sophie. Her sexual appetite kept up with his, and her presence staved off his dreams. Today would be strictly work, not pleasure.

"Hello," Sophie answered abruptly.

"Woah, someone woke up on the wrong side of the bed," he teased. "Stay with me tonight, and I'll make sure it doesn't happen again." The line was cheesy, but he couldn't help himself. She brought it out in him.

"I'm at an open home," she said shortly. "I'm busy. Can I call you later? Or did you want something in particular?"

"No. Just to say hi."

"All right. Bye, then." She hung up.

Cooper stared at the phone, bemused. What the hell was that about? Admittedly, chatting on the phone wasn't part of their arrangement, but he thought they'd more or less tossed out the rule book when she started spending the night with him. He *liked* talking to her, and he missed hearing her voice and seeing her face, even if he'd they'd been apart for less than twenty-four hours. Perhaps he'd overstepped; she might not feel the same way.

Now that he'd stopped to consider it, he realized that she'd been back-pedaling pretty hard since last night. Maybe she was tired of him, even though he hadn't had enough of her yet. His stomach churned nauseatingly, and he rubbed it. God, was she trying to end their fling and he was too dumb to see it? Scowling, he threw the phone at the sofa. If she didn't want to see him anymore, she could damn well tell him to his face.

Cooper fetched the newspaper from his front lawn, shook the dew off and unrolled it on the kitchen table, then scanned the real estate section for open homes. Only two real estate agents worked in Itirangi and they worked for different companies, so it was easy to work out which open home Sophie would be attending. Cooper jotted down the address and grabbed his keys off the hook.

He reached his destination in a few minutes, parked behind Sophie's silver sedan, and checked his watch. She'd be inside for another ten minutes, at least. There was no reason to interfere with her work, so he opened his emails and settled in to wait.

~

SOPHIE WAVED goodbye to the last couple who'd come through the house and locked the door. She'd made it halfway down the path to the gate when she noticed the Ute parked behind her car with a buff blond dude in the driver's seat. She groaned. This couldn't be good. But why oh why did Cooper have to look so danged good being bad?

He hadn't glanced up yet, so she swerved off the path and crossed the lawn to the driveway, hoping to sneak behind him and escape without being noticed. No such luck. She'd just reached for the door when Cooper stepped out of the Ute and crossed his arms over his chest.

"Hey, Soph."

His tone was cheerful; the look in his eyes, not so much. Yeah, she'd been abrupt with him on the phone, but he seemed far angrier than that would warrant. She *was* planning to end things with him, but he couldn't know that. And anyway, it wasn't as if he had any right to be upset under the circumstances.

"Cooper," she replied, tilting her head to acknowledge him.

"Now that you're finished, I thought we could get a bite to eat. I've got an hour to kill before I start work."

"Sorry, can't. I'm meeting Avery. In fact," she said, tapping her watch, "she's probably waiting for me."

"I don't believe you."

Oh. She *was* lying, but she hadn't expected him to call her on it. For a moment, she didn't know how to react. Finally, she said, "That's your prerogative. If you want to think I'm a liar, go for it, but I'm leaving anyway."

He moved more quickly than she thought possible, caging her against the side of the car. "What's going on, Soph?"

His brow was furrowed, his eyes squinty and confused. Her gut plummeted. This was far harder than she'd imagined. Why couldn't he let her bow out gracefully?

"Are you sick of me?" he asked. "Do you not want to see me anymore?"

"No," she croaked, studying the V of his collar rather than meeting his eyes. "I don't."

"But it hasn't been two weeks yet."

"I don't care," she mumbled. "I needed to work Evan out of my system, and I have."

He leaned closer, his breath stirring the hair framing her forehead. "Are you telling me you don't want me anymore?"

She didn't like the tone of his voice. Playful. Challenging. "That's right."

Cooper dropped his hand to caress the side of her neck. Sophie struggled not to turn her face into his palm. Then he leaned in and hovered above her mouth. Unable to resist, she kissed him. Damnation. How could she be so weak that she couldn't even hold out against the subtlest type of torture?

He drew back. "I'm calling bullshit."

"It's not bullshit. I'm tired of you. We had fun, but I'm ready to move on."

Cooper rested his weight on his forearm next to her head, towering over her in a way that was designed to intimidate.

"What the hell is the problem, Sophie? Things have been going great between us, and now, all of a sudden, you want out? I'm not buying it."

"I saw you earlier." She winced at the sound of her voice, unnaturally high. "With your girlfriend and her little girl. Don't play innocent with me, Coop. You're just like every other guy. One woman isn't enough for you."

"What are you talking about?" he demanded.

"I. Saw. You," she enunciated slowly, so he couldn't possibly misinterpret her words. "At the park with that woman and her daughter. I have to say, it's pretty low to cheat on a single mum." She laughed, and the sound was bitter even to her own ears. "And it's a novelty for me, being cast in the role of the other woman. I can't say I like it much."

"Oh." Cooper's expression softened, and he lowered his head towards her. "That's all this is about? It wasn't how it looked, I promise. Just give me a moment to explain."

"I've been here before," she said, holding his gaze, hoping he could see in her eyes how desperately she wanted the chance to lick her wounds in peace. "I'm not about to be taken for a fool again. Leave me alone."

She ducked under his arm and around the side of the car, then jumped into the driver's seat. If he'd wanted to stop her, he could have, but he let her go. As she drove away, she crossed her fingers that he wouldn't make any more fuss. Cooper had helped her move on from Evan, but now she needed to move on from *him*.

She drove to a quiet backstreet, parked the car and drew her knees up to her chest, looped her arms around them and rocked back and forward. She didn't cry. She just sat there until she felt ready to put on a brave face for the world.

CHAPTER 11

Cooper wasn't in the mood for a wedding. He snapped photos, cracked jokes and smiled charmingly, the same as usual, but his heart wasn't in it. For once, the joy of the occasion hadn't rubbed off on him. No, he was dwelling on Sophie—on the sheen of tears in her eyes when she told him she wasn't as I as she used to be.

He'd hurt her. While that had never been his intention, this was new territory for him, and he was only just learning to navigate the terrain. He understood why she'd jumped to the conclusion she had, but it hurt that she'd thought the worst without giving him a chance to explain. He'd never told anyone about Trisha and Madison, so he didn't even know where to start, but she'd made it abundantly clear that if he wanted to be with her, he'd better explain quickly. Otherwise, she might shut him out completely, and he couldn't stand the thought of that.

"Hey, Coop, why the long face?" Brianna, one of the bridesmaids, asked.

"No reason," he replied, embarrassed at being caught mulling over his problems. "Sorry, I was away with the fairies. What were you saying?"

She blinked prettily, eyelashes fluttering. "I was asking if you know of any place where I could stay tonight. I thought I'd booked accommodation, but I got mixed up. Silly me."

Cooper stared blankly. He knew she was angling for an invitation to his place, and not long ago he would have leapt at the opportunity to have an attractive woman fall into his bed so easily, but right now he had more important things on his mind. Besides, Brianna was too tall, her eyes too brown, her hair too pale. Usually, he didn't have a type, but it seemed that short, strawberry-blonde women were growing on him.

"Well?" she prompted.

Cooper fished a business card from his pocket and scribbled a number on the back. "Call this number. It's for a new motel just up the road. I'm sure they'll have something for you." He caught sight of a flash of white in the background. The bride was on the move. "Now, if you'll excuse me."

He brushed past, ignoring the twinge of guilt he felt for rebuffing her attentions. He couldn't be bothered flirting with random women tonight, even for the sake of business. He only wanted one woman, and she wanted nothing to do with him. He needed to tell her about Trisha and Madison, but how? How could he admit to failing his friend, and leaving Ben's soul to walk in the dusty Iranian sun forever? Cooper had survived purely based on luck, but he wasn't whole anymore, and if he opened up to Sophie about Ben, it would mean admitting that.

Perhaps it would be worth it. Sophie was a beautiful, fun woman, a lioness in the sack, and the most giving person he knew. Regardless of his previous reluctance to commit to a woman, he'd be a fool not to hang on to Sophie for as long as the fire blazed between them. At the very least, he couldn't let her go on thinking he was like Evan. He'd never gone behind a woman's back before, not even during a fling. He'd especially never do that to Sophie.

Cooper nodded to himself as he snapped a picture of the

bride silhouetted against the bright light shining through a window, his mind made up. Somehow or another, he had to tell Sophie the truth.

~

Sophie sat cross-legged on the sofa, a bowl of popcorn in her lap and a blanket around her shoulders. She reclined against the cushions, smiling as the opening credits of the TV show *Game of Thrones* started rolling. Her favorite. As she munched on a fistful of popcorn, Cletus curled up next to her and kneaded her thigh, his tail twitching. His needle-like claws pressed into and out of her leg. Sophie tried to ignore the small bursts of pain, but they grew to be too much.

"Cletus," she hissed. "Stop it!"

Cletus stared at her, frozen in place, his ears set back against his head.

"Aw, come on. Don't look at me like I'm the bad guy."

He shoved away from her thigh, sending another jab of pain up her leg, and stalked away.

"You'll be back."

Sophie reached into the popcorn bowl just as someone knocked on the door. Casting a wistful glance at the popcorn, she set it aside, shrugged the blanket off and went to the door. When she yanked it open, her greeting died on her lips at the sight of Cooper on the doorstep, hands in his pockets, his expression inscrutable. Suddenly, she wished she were still dressed for work, or for a date. Anything rather than the loose track pants and knit jersey which probably made her look like someone's virgin aunt or a high school reject.

"What do you want?" she asked tiredly, rubbing her eyes so she didn't have to look at him and his gorgeousness.

"I've—um—got some explaining to do," he said, then glanced past her up the hall. "Can I come in?"

"No." If she let him in, she wouldn't be able to bring herself to kick him out again.

"Okay. I guess that's fair enough." He stepped back and sat on the porch railing, palms resting on his thighs. "There are some things I need to tell you."

Intrigued despite herself, Sophie leaned against the door frame and looked across at him. "Like what?"

His brow furrowed, and his deep blue eyes pierced her to her soul. "This is going to be really hard for me to say. I need to know that you're going to hear me out."

Sophie nodded, although his words had shaken her. This serious, uncertain Cooper wasn't the man she knew, and she wasn't sure how to react to him.

"When we were younger, did you ever meet a guy named Ben Macintosh?" he asked.

The question took her by surprise. It was so seemingly innocuous, so unexpected. "Not that I remember, but I didn't get out much." She'd been too busy working and taking care of Antonia.

"He grew up in Timaru," Cooper continued. Not exactly a local, then, Sophie thought. "He joined the navy at the same time as me. We went through training together and were stationed in the same unit."

The cords of his throat moved as he swallowed. She didn't speak, afraid that if she did, he'd stop confiding in her. He'd never spoken to her about his time in the navy before, and she didn't want to blow it.

"We were friends—best friends," he corrected himself, flushing as though he'd admitted something very personal. "Our tour was almost finished when there was an explosion." He stared into the space somewhere behind her right ear. "A car bomb. I survived, he didn't."

Oh, no. Sophie ached to go to him and provide the comfort he so obviously needed, but she wanted him to finish his story. To tell her how this was relevant to them. "I'm so sorry," she said softly.

"It should have been me." The words were wrenched from him. "Ben had a wife and a baby waiting for him to come home. I had no one."

"That's not true," Sophie interjected. "You had your family."

"But no one who depended on me. Not like that. Before he died, I promised Ben that I'd look after Trisha and Madison, and I have, as best I can. They needed him to come back, but they got me instead."

Suddenly, it all made sense to Sophie. The nightmares. The strange mood he'd been in when he arrived on her doorstep that night. *Survivor's guilt.* Combined with the episodes of PTSD, the emotional baggage he was carrying around must be overwhelming. It was a miracle he managed to get out of bed in the morning, let alone be the charismatic guy he usually was.

Grief was written all over his face, etched in the lines around his mouth. She couldn't bear to see him in such pain. Slowly, so as not to startle him, she crossed the distance between them and wrapped her arms around his waist. They hadn't held each other like this before without it being either the precursor or the aftermath of sex. With every part of her being, she hoped he could sense how grateful she was that *he* had come back from the war. *He* was needed, too.

After a moment, Cooper's arms settled around her and he pulled her close, resting his chin on the top of her head. "The woman from the park," he continued, apparently determined to finish his story.

"Was Ben's wife," Sophie said for him. "I understand. I'm sorry for jumping to conclusions. I just—"

"It's okay," he broke in, stroking her hair. "I don't blame you. I know how it looked, and after what you've been through, I should have told you."

Sophie closed her eyes, enjoying the sensation of his big hands running softly over the back of her head. His unconscious caresses filled her heart to brimming. She'd never felt so cherished before, and so full of admiration for another person. "Thank you for telling me. I feel honored that you trust me enough to be honest."

Cooper shifted on his feet awkwardly. "I wasn't ready for things to be over between us. I hope, now, that we can stay together for a while longer."

The hesitancy in his voice slayed her. "Of course. You don't have any other secrets I should know, do you?"

He huffed in amusement. "Come on, woman. Let a man keep *some* secrets."

"Okay." She laughed against his chest. "As long as those secrets don't affect me, I don't need to hear them. Fair?"

"Fair," he confirmed, releasing her from their hug. He stepped back, hands on her shoulders, to look into her eyes. "Do you have any deep, dark secrets I should know?"

Sophie smiled wryly. "I'm a twenty-five-year-old real estate agent who's never been overseas and still lives where I grew up, with my mother and my cat. I think that about covers it."

"No secret past as a double agent? No crazy exes locked in the attic?"

She laughed, relieved he could joke. "No. I don't have an attic. The basement, on the other hand..."

His eyes widened. "What's in the basement? Do you even have a basement?"

She smirked. "Do I? That's for me to know, and you to wonder about."

"In all seriousness, Soph, what's wrong with your mother?"

Sophie froze, her heat hammering violently in her chest. "When did you see my mother?"

He glanced away guiltily. "I followed you out to her room

one morning. She told me she's terminal. Is it really that bad?"

"She *spoke* to you?"

He acted as if she hadn't said anything. "Don't be mad at me for going behind your back. You would never have told me, otherwise."

He had a point, but it was her right to keep things to herself if she wanted to. Antonia was none of Cooper's business. "You're right," she said. "I wouldn't have told you. Just like you never told me about your nightmares. We all have things we like to keep to ourselves." She paused and took a deep breath. "But tell me, did she really speak to you?"

Cooper stared at her, his brow furrowed, looking perplexed. "Yeah. What's the big deal about that? And how do you know about my nightmares?"

Sophie rolled her eyes impatiently. "Your sister told me. She's my best friend, dumbass."

"Remind me never to trust her again," he muttered.

"Don't hold it against her. You had plenty of opportunities to tell me that the reason you don't like sharing a bed was because you have nightmares. Believe it or not, most women would prefer knowing that to being kicked out with no explanation."

"I don't care what they'd prefer. It's embarrassing. And don't make this about me. I asked about your mother."

Focusing on the first part of what he'd said, Sophie wrapped her arms around him again. When she spoke, her voice was muffled by his shirt. "You have nothing to be embarrassed about. You were brave enough to go to war. Most people can't say that. And the things you went through... Anyone would have nightmares after that."

"Thank you, Soph." His voice was rough, as though he was holding back tears. She squeezed him more tightly and was relieved when he swallowed his pride and hugged her back.

When he finally let go, she screwed up her courage and told him, "Mum has multiple sclerosis. It's a disease that makes the central nervous system shut down. It's slow. She's had it for more than a decade, but she only became unable to walk in the last couple of years. She's depressed, too, which makes it worse."

Sophie drew a shuddering breath. Cooper clasped her to his chest again, and somehow it was easier to talk when she didn't have to look him in the eye. "How do you convince someone to fight for their health when they don't care whether they live or die? I can hardly ever talk her into leaving the bed, and she never leaves the property. She only speaks to me and her nurse, which is why it shocked me that she talked to you."

Cooper's eyebrows shot up. "She never leaves the house? How long has she been that way?"

"Since her speech started to deteriorate. Mum has a lot of pride. When she started feeling like she wasn't in control of her own body, she couldn't bear to let people see her." Sophie could hardly blame her. Antonia had a sharp mind trapped inside a body which continued to let her down.

"How long ago was she diagnosed?"

"A little while after Dad died."

Though she couldn't see his face, she could almost hear his mind whirring as he did the math. "Your dad died when you were really young. How'd you manage?"

The corners of her mouth tightened grimly as she recalled the way she'd scrimped and saved to get by when Antonia could no longer work, then the black pit that had opened up inside her when she realized it would never end. "I applied for a disability benefit on her behalf, and I worked to cover the cost of everything else."

Cooper's fingers tightened on her arm. "Wow. That must have been tough. You were just a kid. I'm sorry. I never knew."

Sophie shrugged a shoulder. "Of course you didn't. I kept it as quiet as possible. Mum wanted it that way. It's not like you could have done anything. No one could."

"You don't know that. Did you get help from anyone? Is she being treated?"

Sophie pushed free, crossed her arms, and scowled at him. "Of course she's being treated. M.S. isn't curable, but she's on medication and gets regular physio." Not that Antonia engaged much. "What, do you think I would let her shut herself away without doing everything I could to help her first? I may have been a kid, but I wasn't stupid. I was desperate to help her. To make her happy." God, how she'd longed to see Antonia smile again, just once. "When we were told there wasn't a cure, I pushed her to attend her physical therapy sessions, take her medication, go out with friends, and keep up her hobbies. If anything, I made it worse, but I still try. One day it might work."

Cooper nodded solemnly. "I know you would have tried everything. You're that kind of person. I'm sorry if it sounded like I was suggesting anything else."

CHAPTER 12

Cooper's gaze tracked down the length of Sophie's body, from her tear-bright eyes to the arms crossed defensively over her chest, to her feet planted firmly on the ground. He rubbed her shoulders gently, wishing his hands were smoother as he worked the tension out of the muscles along the tops of her shoulders and up the sides of her neck. A shaky breath rattled out of her as she dropped her arms and relaxed into his ministrations.

Her eyes drifted closed. "That feels so good."

Her voice was little more than a whisper, but it liquefied his insides, and his fingers trembled against her soft skin. He'd exposed himself tonight, let someone see beneath the surface for the first time in years, and in some twist of fate, he'd seen just as much of her in return. She was as vulnerable as he was, and he could think of nothing but showing her how much he admired her. What an incredible woman she was, taking care of her ill mother, carrying the weight of responsibility from such a young age, and accepting him for who he was without thinking of him as damaged goods.

Sophie's eyes opened, and she blinked slowly. He realized that his hands had stilled on her shoulders and he was staring at her like a creep. Clearing his throat, he dislodged the golf-ball-size lump that seemed to have blocked it, but for the life of him, he couldn't think of the right thing to say.

"Would you like to come in?" Sophie asked, her lips curving into a slight smile.

His heart screamed *yes*. "I'd love to."

Her hands came up to rest on his forearms and she stretched onto her tiptoes as Cooper lowered his head, accepting the blatant invitation to kiss her. He licked the seam of her lips, and as their tongues tangled, a salty-sweet taste exploded in his mouth.

"Popcorn," he murmured, smiling against her lips.

She nodded sheepishly. "You interrupted TV night."

He kissed her again, sliding his hands down her body. With a grunt of effort, he slipped an arm under her bum and lifted her off her feet, then carried her bride-style over the threshold to her bedroom.

He stopped in the doorway, stunned. Clothing, exercise gear, and books were strewn across the floor as if a cyclone had passed through.

"What the hell happened in here?"

Sophie burrowed her face against his chest. "I'm not a very tidy person, okay? If that's a deal-breaker, there's not much I can do about it." She sounded awfully defensive, and with her face hidden from his view, she looked damned adorable.

"You're a cutie," he replied with a chuckle. "You've seen my home. I could use a little chaos in my life."

"Good." Her face re-emerged, and she grinned impishly. "I can arrange that."

She slipped from his arms and leapt up, wrapping her legs around his waist, and planted chaste kisses on his cheeks, forehead, nose and chin. When he closed his eyes beneath her onslaught, she feathered her lips across his eyelids too.

"How are you so amazing?" she murmured.

Gripping her hips, he turned to press her against the wall. "How are you so sexy?"

She smiled coyly. "Tell me, do you make love as well as you flirt?"

"Are you saying you don't know that by now?" Cooper demanded. "What do I need to do to prove it to you?"

He groaned as she took hold of his neck with one hand and reached down to undo his fly with the other. "Maybe just show me one more time."

"Only once more?" His voice became hoarse as she stroked him inside his jeans.

"Maybe twice." A soft breath escaped her as he ground against her, pushing her more tightly against the wall. "God, you can prove it as many times as you like."

Now *that* was what he wanted to hear. Especially when her thready tone spoke of need and she gasped when he kissed her again and again, taking her mouth more fiercely each time. His control was diminishing, and damned if there was a single thing he could do about it. All he wanted was Sophie, naked beneath him, crying his name. Almost losing her had fueled his desperation.

In so many aspects of his life, Cooper was a failure, but he was blessed with the ability to fan the flames of a woman's desire until she became so inarticulate she couldn't even remember her own name. He reminded himself of that now, before he took her like an animal.

His palms cupped her bottom, his fingertips sinking into the perfectly rounded cheeks, and he strode to the bed and laid her down. He stepped back to undress, smirking when she pulled a face at him.

"Hurry up and get back here," she ordered.

"Be patient," he replied, slowing his pace, undoing his shirt one button at a time. Her increasingly shallow breaths showed how much she appreciated his efforts. "I'll be worth the wait, I promise."

But no, his Sophie didn't have a single shred of patience. Instead of watching the show as he'd intended, she put on one of her own, wriggling out of her pants and top so she was naked except for a pair of flesh-toned lace panties with red bows at the hips. A pretty package for him to unwrap. Her knees fell apart, exposing her fully to his view, and she laid her hand over her sex and rubbed up and down slowly, waiting for him to react.

Cooper had never seen anything so erotic in his life. For a long moment, he stared, unable to move, unable to speak. Then he remembered himself, and without taking his eyes away from her, he shook his jeans off, dropped his underwear to the ground, and took himself in his hand. He gave himself a long stroke, pretending it was Sophie's dainty hand wrapped around him rather than his own large, clumsy one. Eyes glued to her, he noticed her clever fingers fumble.

Gotcha. "Two can play at that game, Soph."

Her lips parted, and her tongue darted forward to wet them. The glimpse of pink made him even harder, if that was possible. "I play it better," she said huskily.

"Wanna bet?" He stroked himself again, suppressing a shudder, not wanting her to know how close he was to the brink.

"What odds?" She sucked a finger into her mouth right up to the knuckle and pulled it free with a pop.

Cooper pictured her making the same motion with something other than her finger. "Loser buys dinner sometime this week."

He'd intended to say something kinkier, but for some reason, the thought of a simple dinner with her appealed to him.

Sophie nodded. "Whoever comes first, loses."

He could listen to vulgar words come out of her mouth all day. "Deal. But do me a favor. Say that again."

Her eyes widened in surprise, then darkened with understanding. "Whoever comes first, loses. Go on, you know you want to come, Coop. Come for me."

He groaned. She smiled with satisfaction and drew her panties to the side, slid the finger she'd sucked back and forth over her clit, then slipped it inside herself. She closed her eyes, her face a mask of pleasure, and Cooper wished he were the one giving her that pleasure.

"Open your eyes," he ordered. "I want you to see what you're doing to me."

She opened them and fixated on his hand as he pumped up and down. His shaft leapt in his palm as her eyes grew hungry, and the harsh sounds of their breathing filled the room. Cooper was close. He could feel the orgasm sneaking up on him, but Sophie was close too. He could see it in her eyes and in the way her chest rose and fell with each labored breath. Gritting his teeth, he focused on holding out a little longer, but then Sophie bit her lip and sent him over the edge. His whole body shook with the force of his climax, and he fought to keep his eyes open so he could watch as Sophie followed him to the peak of bliss, then finally collapsed back against the bed, sated.

He staggered over, legs trembling beneath his weight, and flopped next to her. "Wow."

"Mm-hmm," she murmured drowsily, rolling over to fling an arm across his chest. "I agree."

"I've never come so hard without someone else touching me," he confessed, sliding an arm under her shoulders and dragging her closer so he could kiss the top of her head, the strands of hair like silk against his cheek. "Is this normal for you?"

"Totally normal."

His heart stuttered. "*What?*"

"Relax, big guy," she said with a soft chuckle. "I was kidding. No, it's never been like this."

"Thank God." Relief coursed through his veins. He

couldn't stomach the thought of her being less affected by their chemistry than he was, or that she might have done this all before with someone else. Someone like that smarmy lawyer.

Once upon a time, this closeness between them would have unsettled him, but now he craved it. He could imagine craving it forever.

~

As the warmth leached from her body, Sophie wriggled closer to Cooper and laid her head on his chest, then listened to the soft thud of his heart, delighting in the sensation of his breath stirring her hair. She felt utterly at peace, pressed up against his big body. With Cooper, she'd begun to discover that she could be naked and totally exposed but still feel secure and confident in herself. As he used his strong forearm to tug her closer, her heart sang out and goosebumps skittered over her skin. She could think of nowhere she'd rather be, and no one she'd rather be with.

It would be so easy to fall in love with him. He clearly wasn't ready to part with her; otherwise, he would have let her walk away without ripping the scab off an old wound. He definitely cared, but would it be enough?

She put the thought to the back of her mind. Right now, he was hers, and she focused on that.

"You know, Soph," Cooper began, the vibrations of his voice rumbling under her cheek, "maybe we could—"

Beep! A piercing noise cut him off.

"What's that?" he asked, but she was already up and digging through her clothes on the floor, withdrawing the monitor from a pocket. Ignoring him, she flicked it on and it started flashing, with *Low Heart Rate Alert* written across the screen.

She scrolled across to see what the heart rate reading was and gasped. "Oh my God."

It had never been so low, even in the deepest of sleeps—and Antonia slept very deeply because of the pills she was on. Sophie scrambled to her feet, yanked an overlong hoodie over her head and ran for the door, calling back over her shoulder, "Something is wrong with Mum."

If anything had happened to her while Sophie had been fooling around with Cooper, she'd never forgive herself. It was her responsibility to keep her mother as healthy as possible.

She crossed the yard to the Big House, sure-footed in the dark, and threw the door open. Whitney Houston's "I Will Always Love You" was playing softly in the background, sending a chill up her spine. The light in Antonia's bedroom was off, so Sophie fumbled to find the switch. When light flooded the room, it cast the horrific scene before her into sharp relief.

Antonia lay sprawled on the pillows, mouth hanging open, a pill bottle on her lap and a few pills scattered where her hand had fallen at her side. Sophie raced over, snatched the bottle up and swore. Sleeping pills. Last night there had been at least a couple weeks' worth, and now the bottle was empty save for the pills on the bed.

A sharp intake of breath sounded behind her, and Sophie swung around to see Cooper standing at the door. "Have you got your phone?" she demanded. He nodded. "Call one-one-one."

While he spoke to an operator, Sophie tuned him out, counting the pills so she knew how many had been taken. Then she moved Antonia's limp body into the rescue position, unsure if it would help, but she had to do *something.*

Cooper hung up. "There's an ambulance on the way," he said, tossing her a pair of jeans.

Sophie put them on and leaned over to listen to her

mother's shallow breathing. She didn't know anything about drug overdoses, but this looked bad to her. "They goddamn better hurry." She grabbed Antonia's hand, which was cold and clammy to the touch. "I can't lose her."

THE AMBULANCE ARRIVED ten minutes after Cooper had called for help, during which time Antonia had become increasing cold and still. At first, she groaned occasionally and twitched, but the signs of life became less regular while they waited. After she'd been loaded into the ambulance, Sophie got in behind, unwilling to leave her side.

"I'll follow you to the hospital," Cooper said before the doors closed between them.

When his face was gone from view, Sophie slumped against the bench on the inside wall of the ambulance and clasped her hands together. When they began to shake, she sat on them.

"Will she be okay?" she asked the paramedic, a thin guy who looked to be in his fifties.

He glanced over. "Too early to say, but we'll do everything we can. Once she's at the hospital, the doctors can pump her stomach."

"She should have a tolerance," Sophie said. "That will help, right? Because it would take more pills to have an effect?"

"It's possible. Just sit tight. We'll do what we can."

Sophie swallowed the dozen or so questions she still had, biting down on her tongue to keep her panic under control. Now wasn't the time. She had to let the paramedic do his job.

The ambulance had no windows, so she couldn't watch the scenery to distract herself. Instead, she focused on her mother's legs. They were spindly, the muscles atrophied from lack of use despite the exercises Sophie and the physio had guided Antonia through. Sophie's best effort had been too little to make a difference. Her legs were smooth, though, and her toenails were painted pink. Antonia had always tended towards vanity, so Sophie had made sure the nurse helped her shave, instigated a skin-care regime, and spritzed her wrist with the expensive Yves Saint Laurent perfume she adored. Sophie had always thought it was important that Antonia feel well-groomed, so that maybe one day she'd be struck by the whim to go to town. See the world again. It seemed she'd been hoping in vain. Her mother would never be ready to rejoin the world. On the contrary, it seemed she was determined to leave it. *But why?* What had happened, what had Sophie done, to make her mother decide that she couldn't go on?

Tears prickled her eyes. Sophie squeezed them shut, and a single tear trickled down her cheek and dripped off her chin as she took a deep breath. It wasn't over yet. They could survive this.

She wiped her damp cheek with the back of her sleeve and opened her eyes, her vision now blurry. She blinked the unshed tears back, and everything came back into focus. She couldn't be weak now.

Pull it together, girl.

Traffic noises heralded their arrival in Timaru. Only a few miles left to the hospital. They'd nearly made it.

Hold on, Mum.

Cooper followed close behind the ambulance, but before long, it was out of sight. Unfortunately, he had to obey the speed laws, and the ambulance didn't. Regardless, he drove towards Timaru as fast as he legally could. Sophie had been there for him when he needed it, and now she needed him to be there for her. He couldn't let her down. He owed his current happiness, and his optimism for the future, to her.

For the first time since his return from the war, the prospect of night didn't frighten him. He didn't feel loneliness crushing the spirit out of him, and it was all thanks to her.

As he came into Timaru, it seemed every traffic light changed to red a moment before he arrived. He scowled darkly as a woman pushed a stroller across the street in front of him, forcing him to slow down. She smiled and waved cheerfully. Cooper gritted his teeth and counted to three, his mind going back to the moment when he'd seen Antonia unconscious on the bed, sleeping pills scattered over her lap. Was this the first time she'd tried to kill herself, or was it part of a pattern? For Sophie's sake, he hoped not.

Finally, the hospital came into view. It was an ugly block that seemed to squat by the roadside, a Frankenstein's monster of a building, a mish-mash of architecture from different decades when additional wings had been added on as needed. The parking lot was full, so Cooper parked on the side of the road and jogged to the main entrance, pausing between the two sets of automatic glass doors to sanitize his hands. He stopped in front of the receptionist's booth and waited for her to finish filling in a form.

"I'm looking for Antonia Delaware," he said.

The receptionist adjusted the oval spectacles perched on her nose and peered closely at her computer screen. "Third floor," she told him. "Room 309." He started towards the stairs, but the receptionist called after him, "It's family only at the moment, sir."

"I am family," he replied. "She's my mother-in-law."

He hoped she hadn't noticed the lack of a ring on his finger, but she didn't ask any further questions, so he carried on up the stairs. When he reached the third floor, he hurried around the corner, dodging a doctor coming in the other direction. He counted the rooms, arrived at the one labeled '309' and peered through a small panel window. People in scrubs were clustered around a stretcher bed, and he couldn't see past them.

He paused with a hand on the door, posed to push it open. Was it really his place to enter? Did he have the right to be present at a time like this?

A movement at the side of the room caught his attention, and he finally noticed Sophie sitting on the floor, her arms looped around her knees, drawing them tightly to her chest. At the sight of her, so small and vulnerable, his chest ached for her, and he remembered why he'd come. Pushing the door open, he slipped into the room as unobtrusively as possible and sat next to Sophie, putting an arm around her narrow shoulders.

"It's all right," he murmured in her ear, then pressed his lips to the side of her head. "She's going to be fine."

"You can't promise that," Sophie whispered.

Her knuckles were white where she was clutching her legs. Every part of her was tense. Cooper wished he could do something more for her, but all he could offer were empty words of comfort. The trouble was, she could see right through him.

"No," he replied softly. "I can't. I'm sorry. But I promise I'll be here for you no matter what."

For a long moment, she was silent. He feared he might have overstepped, but then she spoke. "Thank you."

While it wasn't the most articulate or poetic of responses, to Cooper, it felt profound. She'd accepted what little support he could offer. He nestled closer to her, and together they watched the medical professionals work, praying for a good outcome.

CHAPTER 13

After an excruciating wait, a doctor approached Sophie, who was still huddled against the wall with Cooper.

"Your mother is stable," he said with a small smile. "We're not out of the woods yet, but I'm cautiously optimistic that she can make it through this."

Sophie nodded. This meant her prayers had been answered, though everything was happening so quickly, she'd barely processed any of it. By the time she woke tomorrow, she had no doubt that the events of today would finally have sunk in, but in the meantime, she felt like she was in a trance.

"Thanks, Doctor," Cooper said when she didn't respond. "Will she need to stay the night?"

"At this point, I think Mrs. Delaware will need to stay at least tonight, possibly tomorrow as well, and we'll need to consider putting her on suicide watch."

He thought she'd try again? Sophie picked at the quick of her fingernails. She'd known for years that her mother was depressed, but she'd been on anti-depressants, and Sophie had never dreamed she was suicidal. Why hadn't she made an attempt on her life before now? Sophie couldn't think of anything that would have triggered it.

"Please." Sophie spoke before she even realized she meant to. "Put Mum on suicide watch. I couldn't handle it if..." Her throat closed up and her chin wobbled, making it difficult to speak. She cleared her throat, and the sound was harsh in the quiet room. "If she tried this again," she continued, "I don't know what I'd do."

The doctor looked at her sympathetically, then summoned one of the nurses, a young man in blue scrubs. "Ms. Delaware, I'd like you to go with Jason. He can talk you through some options."

"Options?"

"For getting your mother the help she needs."

Sophie inhaled deeply and got to her feet. "Okay."

Cooper rested his hand on her elbow as they followed Jason to an office tucked away behind the waiting room. Having Cooper's solid presence beside her was reassuring, like she could turn and lean on him if she needed to. But then, before they sat, he let her go, kissed her cheek, and said, "Are you okay if I leave you for a while? I have a few things to take care of."

"Of course," Sophie replied numbly. She was engulfed by a blank, hollow feeling as he left her side, as if he were ripping part of her away with him.

"I'll be back for you," he said. "I promise. Trust me."

His gorgeous eyes willed her to believe him, so she did. She stepped into his embrace and went up on tiptoe to whisper in his ear. "I trust you. Just don't let me down."

"I won't." He kissed her again, this time on the lips, and walked away.

Sophie sat and faced the nurse, Jason. "So, what are my options?"

He picked up a notepad and pen. "There are a few. But

first, I have some questions. Your mother is on antidepressants?"

"Yes, some pretty potent ones, I think."

"Sleeping pills, too?"

"Yes. She's also on immunosuppressants and steroids for her M.S."

Jason nodded, scribbling on his notepad. "Has she ever tried to commit suicide before?"

"No. At least, not that I'm aware of." Could it be possible that she had, and Sophie had been none the wiser?

"Does she see a counsellor?"

"No, but she talks to the nurse who takes care of her. At least, as much as she really talks to anyone."

"Have you tried counselling before?"

"Years ago, but Mum refused to talk. She doesn't speak now to anyone except for me and her nurse."

He jotted a few more notes. "She doesn't see friends?"

Sophie closed her eyes, embarrassed to admit the truth when it made her feel like such a failure. "She doesn't really have any friends left."

Jason raised an eyebrow. "How long has she been this bad?"

"Years." She couldn't believe she was rehashing this for the second time in a day. "Back when she started to go downhill, I tried everything I could think of to improve her mood, but nothing seemed to help. The worse the M.S. symptoms got, the blacker her mood got. She never said anything about being suicidal, though, and she didn't seem to be doing anything out of character recently, except..."

"Except what?" he prompted.

She frowned. "It's probably nothing."

Tapping his pen against his chin, he pinned her with a gaze. "Ms. Delaware, the smallest detail can be what pieces things together."

"She talked to the man I'm dating, which is pretty unusual

for her. I would have expected her to withdraw into herself rather than speak with him when he visited her. Does that mean anything?"

"It could do. It's hard to know."

Frustration bubbled through Sophie. It seemed like for every answer, two more questions were raised.

"So, would you say the M.S. was what triggered the depression?"

Sophie considered it. "After my dad died, she grieved for a long time. She'd almost come out of it when she was diagnosed with M.S. The symptoms weren't bad at first, but it got worse and worse. After a couple of years, she was also diagnosed with depression. So, yeah, that could be the case. She went from working full-time and having a busy social life to not leaving the house except in emergencies, and then one day, she just wouldn't get out of bed. The physiotherapist does some exercises with her, and so do I, but I don't know how effective they are."

He was nodding, rubbing his chin thoughtfully with his thumb. "Does she read? Watch TV? Do any crafts?"

"She watches TV sometimes, when I put it on for her. I try to encourage her to read, but I don't think she ever does. No crafts. Most of the time, she just listens to music."

Jason scrawled a couple of bullet points and placed the notepad on the desk, then gave Sophie his full attention. "Can I speak frankly?"

"Of course."

"Your mother is one of the worst cases I've ever seen. Personally, I'd recommend that you check her in to the Mental Health and Addiction Center. You can't watch her all of the time, and it doesn't seem as if she has anything but time to sit around and convince herself to try again. What do you think?"

What did she *think*? Sophie's brain still hadn't caught up. Her thoughts were whizzing all over the place, and she couldn't focus on any of them except for an overwhelming sense that everything was about to come crashing down around her.

"Would they..." she began, then her voice broke. She cleared her throat and tried again. "Would they have the right facilities to look after her? Mum isn't very independent. She needs a lot of assistance."

"They cater to a wide range of people. I'm sure they could formulate a plan for your mum."

"How long would it be for?" She felt guilty even considering the idea. She didn't want Antonia to think she was washing her hands of her.

"Anywhere from a couple of weeks to several months, depending on what the therapists at the center advise."

"Is it expensive?" God knew her budget was limited.

"It's very case-specific. If you were to finance it yourself, it could be expensive, but I believe Antonia would qualify for a subsidy, and since she'd be referred by a doctor, the cost would be lower. I really couldn't estimate a cost myself. You should book an appointment with the center and discuss the details with them, then make up your mind about it."

"Thanks for your advice," Sophie said. "I'll think about it."

"Good." Jason glanced down at his notes again. "Shall we return and see how she's doing?"

"Yes, please."

SOPHIE SAT vigil by Antonia's bedside, watching her sleep until the attending physician urged her to go home and rest.

"I doubt her condition will change tonight," he said. "There's no point in you staying here and wearing yourself out."

She hesitated, feeling as if she'd be betraying her mum by going home.

"I don't want another patient on my hands," the doctor added. "Go on."

Wearily, she stood, rubbed her eyes and stretched the kinks out of her back. She wandered down the halls and three flights of stairs to the exit. Then she paused as realization hit her. She'd ridden here in the ambulance. She had no way home.

She slumped against the wall with a thump. She'd just have to stay, unless Cooper was still in town. She selected his number on her phone, and her finger hovered over the call button as she debated whether to call him. He hadn't returned to the hospital yet. She didn't want to read anything into that, but it didn't bode well. Then her desire for sleep overcame her desire to avoid rejection. Biting her lip, she called him.

One ring, two rings, three rings; she was beginning to second-guess herself when he answered. "Hey, Soph."

"Hey," she replied softly, then stopped, not knowing how to continue. She didn't want to ask too much of him, but he *had* said to trust him. "I'm, um, finished at the hospital. Are you still around?"

"I am," he said. "I'll be there in five minutes, okay?"

She breathed a sigh of relief. "Thank you."

"Any time, babe."

After they hung up, she found a chair near the exit and waited, watching the minutes tick over on her phone. Finally, her phone buzzed, signaling an incoming text message.

I'm outside.

Pocketing her phone, she walked out, shivering when a cool breeze ruffled her hair. She spotted Cooper immediately, waiting in a no-park zone near the entrance. He smiled tentatively, as if he was unsure whether smiling was appropriate.

Sophie hopped into the passenger seat, her stomach grumbling hungrily when she smelled Indian takeaways. He must have eaten recently. She wondered if there were any leftovers. "Thank you so much."

"No worries. I told you I'd come back for you, Soph, and I meant it. How is she?"

"Sleeping without a care in the world." If she sounded bitter, good. She felt it. "Where did you go?"

Cooper wiped his palms on his jeans before taking hold of the steering wheel to pull away from the curb. "You know how I told you about my friend Ben's wife, Trisha?"

A chill ran up her back. "Yeah, but what does that have to do with anything?"

"Trisha is a doctor. She works at a private medical center that trials new therapies for treating mental illnesses."

The tension seeped out of her spine. "New therapies? Like, experimental ones?"

Cooper made a sound of disagreement in the back of his throat. "Experimental only in one sense of the word. They're techniques which aren't mainstream yet. Trisha and her colleagues are working to make them more mainstream by documenting each patient who undergoes one of the treatments and recording the result. For the most part, the treatments don't involve any medication. They're purely behavioral."

"Okay, I think I'm following you."

"I visited Trisha to talk about your mum and whether any of their treatments might work for her."

"That's thoughtful." And totally presumptuous. Feelings of gratitude and annoyance swirled within her. Unsure which was the dominant emotion, she opted to ignore them both and press forward. "What did she say?"

"That you wouldn't appreciate me interfering." He glanced over at her with a wry expression. "But they have a new program which might suit your mum, and if you're interested, you should call Trisha."

He reached into the ashtray, withdrew a business card

and handed it to her. Sophie skimmed the details and slipped it carefully into her purse. After her discussion with Jason at the hospital, she was definitely open to trying something new.

"For what it's worth, whether I'm interfering or not, I think you should call her," Cooper continued. "They do some great things at the center. I think they could really help your mum."

While he was, indeed, interfering, it had been a long time since anyone had cared enough to interfere with Sophie's affairs, and the fact that he had brought tears to her eyes. If she'd had any remaining thoughts that she was just a fling to him, they were gone.

He cares.

Impulsively, Sophie clasped his left hand in both of hers and kissed it.

"Thank you," she said. "*Thank you.* I'll call her."

The side of his mouth slanted into a bemused smile. "Let me know if there's anything else I can do to help. I want to be here for you."

~

SHE LOOKS WIPED OUT.

Cooper studied Sophie surreptitiously during the drive to her home. The color had leached from her skin over the course of the night until it was even paler than usual, and her freckles stood out starkly in contrast. Her eyes looked sunken, with dark smudges visible beneath them, and her shoulders were hunched forward. Cooper's fingers twitched on the steering wheel, itching to fold her into a hug and smooth the creases on her forehead. Instead, he tightened his grip and focused on getting them home quickly.

Though it was pitch black outside, Sophie was staring out the window, apparently deep in thought. Today must have been hard for her, and he hoped that he'd made it easier in some small way.

When he parked outside her house and opened his car door, Sophie looked over, eyebrows raised. "You're coming in?"

"Of course." As if he would abandon her at a time like this. He got out of the car quickly, opened the door to the back seat and retrieved the containers of Indian takeout and the bottle of wine.

Sophie got out too, and her eyes widened as they alighted on the food. "Is that for me?"

"For both of us," he clarified. Damned if he was going to go hungry. "The wine is all yours."

The corner of her mouth lifted. "I promise not to threaten you with it."

Tenderness welled up within him. "Good. Now, get your sexy little butt inside, put on your pajamas, and I'll bring you food."

"Seriously?" She looked like she was waiting to hear the catch.

"Seriously."

"Thanks."

Her lips parted as if she wanted to say something more, but then she shook her head and turned away, opened the front door of her house, and headed directly for her bedroom.

Cooper made his way down the hall and into the living room, where he switched on the light so he wouldn't stumble over the cat bed in the center of the floor or the washing rack against the wall. He searched the kitchen cupboards until he found bowls, and evenly divvied the butter chicken between two of them. He poured Sophie a generous glass of wine and helped himself to a can of beer from the fridge.

While he began to carry their dinner to the living room, Sophie waited on the sofa wearing a pair of polar fleece pajamas, with her feet tucked underneath her. Cooper paused to drink in the sight. Two weeks ago, he never would have imagined that the sight of a fully clothed, exhausted woman could appeal to him. Now, he found it strangely stirring. Not sexually, but emotionally. Flutters began in the vicinity of his heart, an organ he'd long thought was dormant.

"Coop, you okay?"

Jolted from his reverie, he blinked rapidly and handed her a bowl of curry and naan bread, hoping to cover his distraction. He expected her to insist that he tell her what he'd been thinking about—many of his exes would have, and Sophie had shown that she could be a tenacious bulldog at times—but instead, she just used the naan bread to scoop a generous dollop of curry into her mouth.

Cooper lowered himself cautiously to the sofa beside her, doing his best not to disrupt her comfortable position. He hadn't realized how hungry he was until he began to eat. He plowed through his curry in a matter of minutes and looked longingly at hers.

"I should've bought two," he muttered under his breath.

Sophie, noticing his distress, broke off part of her naan bread and offered it to him.

"No, no," he replied, waving his hand. "I couldn't. That's yours."

"Are you sure?" she asked, waving it under his nose. "It's so tasty."

She bit off a mouthful and chewed it slowly, closing her eyes in bliss. Cooper leaned over and kissed her closed lips, and her eyes shot open, cloudy with confusion and something else. Rather than ponder what it was, he took the naan bread from her and ruffled her hair, setting a few reddish-blonde strands loose around her face.

"Thanks, Soph."

"No problem." She patted his stomach. "We've got to keep the beast fed."

"Are you calling me a beast?" he teased.

"I meant the beast inside your belly," she explained. "I heard it growling earlier."

He had no reply for that. It was true, he had a very vocal gut.

After Sophie had finished her dinner, she rested on the sofa, her eyelashes casting shadows over her cheeks. Cooper suspected she was mulling things over, analyzing them to death. But enough of that. He collected their dishes and left them on the kitchen counter. When he returned, he held out a hand out to Sophie, pulled her into his embrace and breathed in the sweet scent of her. Banding his arm around her upper back, he drew her so close that it was difficult to tell where he ended and she began, then closed his eyes and let himself swim in the sensation of being one with her.

She fit against him so perfectly. Short where he was tall. Slim where he was bulky. But he knew she wouldn't break if he were clumsy with her. His Sophie was strong, too. If he could take her pain and absorb it into himself, he would, without a second thought.

Slowly, he released her and cleared his throat. What was it with all of these sentimental thoughts? He was becoming soft.

"Hey, Shorty," he said gruffly. "Why don't you get ready for bed? I'll join you in a few minutes."

"Sure." She smiled, and he turned to mush on the inside. It would take more than a few minutes to regain his composure.

~

Sophie stretched towards the ceiling, her entire body tense—one of the effects of too much adrenaline, she supposed. She shrugged her shoulders backwards, trying to loosen the muscles in her neck and shoulders.

"Are you sore?" Cooper asked.

"A little," she admitted.

A moment later, she felt his presence at her back, and his hands settled on her hips. She relaxed against him, his body offering her a haven of comfort, and turned her face up towards his. He kissed her chastely, then scooped her off her feet and laid her on the bed. Before she could protest, he stripped her shirt off and dropped it on the floor.

"Hang on," she began. "I'm not exactly—"

"It's okay," he soothed. "I'm not after sex. If you lie face-down, I'll massage you."

"Oh." Well, she'd be a fool to argue against a massage. She reached around and undid her bra strap so it wasn't a barrier. "Thank you. There's oil on the bedside table."

She heard him grumble, "There's a whole lot on the bedside table."

She would have laughed if she'd had the energy. Instead, she murmured her agreement. "I'm a mess. Sorry."

"You're *my* mess. This will probably be a little cold."

Sophie shivered as a splash of oil landed on her back. Before it could slide off, Cooper caught it with one of his fingers and turned the motion into a caress, his hand gliding along the side of her body, up her ribs and over her shoulders. For someone who took photographs for a living, his hands were rough, creating a divine friction as they moved up and down her back, into the indentation of her spine and the groove between her shoulder blades. Warmth from his hands infused her, softening the muscles of her upper back. A sound of satisfaction escaped her as he pressed his fingers into a knot and kneaded it out. Then his hands swept down to where her back swayed inward, and he stroked the muscles bordering her spine with his thumb.

Sophie focused on the sensations radiating out from his touch. She'd never had a massage she hadn't paid for. None of her previous lovers had thought it was necessary. Their needs were purely sexual, and they assumed hers were too. She'd never known any different, but now she realized how wrong they had been. Having someone touch her body so tenderly without expecting any sexual favors in return was perhaps the sweetest thing she'd ever experienced. She felt cherished. She knew it was foolish, but she was too tired to resist the emotions crashing through her, and her heart couldn't be dissuaded. Sighing in pleasure, she stopped thinking at all, absorbed in the way Cooper was touching her body exactly how she needed it most. Soon, she was beyond noticing anything, and she drifted off to sleep.

CHAPTER 14

Sophie was hovering at the kitchen door, watching Cooper with an expression that was somewhere between bewildered and exasperated. "Are you sure I can't help?"

Cooper waved her away. "Go get dressed, Shorty. I can handle things in here."

She lingered in the doorway for a moment longer before she left, muttering about how he'd taken over her home. Grinning, Cooper flipped a pancake and hummed under his breath. He shifted the bacon so it didn't burn the bottom of the frying pan and glanced inside the oven to check on the hash browns.

Sophie had been out of sorts since she woke, endearingly grumpy, with mussed hair that resembled a troll doll's. She didn't know how to hand control over to someone else, but he was determined to teach her. It wasn't fair that she'd been responsible for so much and seemed not to expect any better. He planned to show her how nice it could be if someone else looked after her for a while.

Fetching a couple of plates from the cupboard, Cooper nearly tripped over a fat tabby cat that wound between his feet and meowed piercingly. He glared down at it, and it stared back, tail twitching.

"What's your problem, cat?" he demanded.

"His name is Cletus," Sophie called from the other room. "Come here, puss-puss-puss."

The cat's eyes darted towards the door and back to Cooper, and Cooper could have sworn they narrowed. Then the cat took off, presumably in favor of cuddles from Sophie. Smart cat.

"Cletus?" he asked.

Her laugh was musical. "Don't blame me. He used to belong to Avery. She named him."

"Did she hate his guts?"

"Yeah. She's not a cat person."

"Still, that's a whole other level of cruel." Although the squinty-eyed creature might deserve it. Cooper piled food onto the plates, carried them from the kitchen, and, with a flourish, presented one to Sophie, who was seated on the couch in the living room. "Your breakfast is served, milady."

Her eyes widened. "Wow. Are you trying to fatten me up?"

He shrugged as he sat down beside her. "You could use a good meal. Dig in."

Sophie skewered a piece of pancake drizzled with maple syrup and moaned as she chewed it. "Damn, that's good," she said, then licked a crumb from her lip. "Where did you learn to cook?"

"I have to cook for myself at home," he replied once he'd swallowed a mouthful of bacon. "Most mornings I work from there, so I have plenty of time to play around in the kitchen."

Sophie smiled. "Cooper Simons, master chef. Who knew?"

"I guess it runs in the family." His sister, Aria, could bake a mean cake, and regularly cooked for fundraisers and other community events.

Sophie laid down her cutlery and looked at him with a curious expression, her head tilted to the side, a crinkle forming between her eyebrows. "Coop, I don't get it. Why are you being so nice to me? How come you're still here?"

Her questions weren't entirely unexpected. Clearly, something had been brewing in her mind all morning.

"Why does it surprise you? It shouldn't, Soph. I told you yesterday that I'm not ready for us to be over. Right now, you need me. So here I am."

"But you don't have to stay here and deal with my bull-shit." Her lips pursed in bemusement. "That's not what you signed up for."

"I know I don't *have* to," he explained. "I want to. You deserve to be treated properly and taken care of."

Frustration simmered inside him and he rubbed his chin, hearing the rasp of his stubble against his thumb. His other hand fisted around the hilt of his knife, and he laid it down carefully. Damn it all to hell. How had Sophie gotten to this point in her life without learning to expect some basic human decency?

"The men you've dated have been idiots if they haven't seen you for the treasure you are. God, you shouldn't have to be suspicious of my motives. This is what people in a normal, caring relationship do for each other."

Her face blanched. "*Are* we in a relationship?"

He groaned. Poor word choice. "We don't need to label it. That's not the point. What matters is that I'm here for you."

He heard Sophie's quick intake of breath. "I think I do need a label." Her voice had trembled, and she made a visible effort to meet his gaze. "I'm getting too attached to you," she admitted, and he could see it cost her. "If our affair is only short-term, I think we need to end it now. I don't want you to break my heart."

It felt like she'd stabbed him through the heart with an icicle. Cold permeated his chest from the invisible wound and he jolted, forgetting the plate of breakfast on his lap until it toppled to the floor. Sophie squealed in shock, but he didn't care. He dropped to his knees before her and shook his head.

"No!"

His exclamation rang out in the silence of the house. He'd won her back yesterday, and he wasn't about to let her go now. Cletus leapt to his feet, hissing, and stalked out of the room, but Cooper ignored him. He grabbed Sophie's hands and tucked them under his chin. "I won't break your heart, Sophie," he vowed. If he became another name on the list of sad sacks who'd short-changed her, he'd kick his own ass. "Please, just give me a chance to be the man you deserve. I don't know if it'll work out, but let me try."

"Long-term?" she asked skeptically. "Are you really capable of that?"

Her doubt seared him. "I don't know," he said, hoping his honesty wouldn't cost him. "But for the first time ever, I want to find out." He uncurled her fingers and kissed her palm. "Come on, Soph. Throw me a bone, here. I'm on my knees for you. Do you want me to beg? I will."

A million thoughts flashed through her expressive blue-green eyes. Cooper forced himself to remain silent so she could arrive at a decision on her own.

"Okay," she said finally, her eyes glittering. "But don't make me regret it."

"I won't," he promised, climbing back up onto the couch so he could capture her mouth. "Come to dinner at Aria's with me tonight," he said impulsively. "As my girlfriend."

She stiffened, and he winced. Had he pushed for too much too soon? Then she sucked her bottom lip into her mouth and released it with a popping sound. Cooper hissed low, unable to tear his gaze from her plump lips.

"Fine." Her voice was so soft, he had to struggle to hear it. "But first, we need to clean up in here, we need to visit Mum, and," she said, her eyes darkening to the color of a stormy sea, "you need to make love to me until I can't think straight. Can you do that?"

Every part of him stood at attention. "Damn right, I can."

~

"WHAT WERE YOU THINKING?" Sophie demanded of Antonia, who was reclining on a hospital bed, wearing a blue gown and an indignant expression.

"I was thinking of you," Antonia replied, enunciating her words carefully. Ironically, this was the liveliest Sophie had seen her in months.

"Of *me*? Why in God's name would you think I'd want you to die?"

"I didn't think that," Antonia said haltingly. "I thought if I was gone, you could live your life freely." Her eyes began to water, and Sophie clasped her hand, feeling guilty for interrogating someone who was clearly unwell. "You're such a good girl," Antonia continued, "and I'm—" She sighed. "I'm just a...a...broken-down, silly old goose."

Sophie lay down next to her mum on the bed. "You *are* a silly old goose," she agreed. "You gave me the fright of my life. Please don't ever do that again. I'd never be happier in a world without you in it, okay?"

"Okay." Antonia's response was meek as a newborn kitten's.

Sophie turned her head to see that tears were spilling down her mother's cheeks. "Oh, Mum." She pulled Antonia's head over to rest on her shoulder. "I love you."

"Love you too, Sweets."

Sophie sniffled. 'Sweets' was the nickname her father had given her. Neither she nor her mother had uttered it once since he'd passed. Her heart lifted just a little. Finally, after years of hoping and praying, she'd seen an ounce of progress, enough to give her hope for the future. If therapy worked, maybe she'd see Antonia dress like a queen and roll through the streets of Itirangi again, or hear her voice fill the air with music. Maybe she could have a family again.

On that note…

"You know how I was having a fling with Cooper Simons?"

"Hmm, yes. He's very handsome."

A laugh gurgled up Sophie's throat and burst out, sounding two parts happy and one part sad. No matter what state Antonia was in, she'd always appreciated a fine specimen of a man.

"Yeah, he is, isn't he? And we're dating, Mum. Dating properly."

"Good."

She sounded so satisfied that Sophie craned her neck around to look at her fully. "You sound happy."

Antonia nodded. "Because *you're* happy. That's all I want. That Evan…" She grimaced, her droopy cheeks distorting her face. "He wasn't good enough for you. But this one, I like."

The corners of her mouth twitched upwards. It wasn't quite a smile, but damned if it wasn't the closest to one that Sophie had seen in a long time.

"I'm glad you approve."

A nurse knocked on the door. "Mrs. Delaware?" she asked.

Sophie waved her into the room. "I should be going." She climbed off the bed, then leaned down and kissed Antonia's cheek. "I'll be back tomorrow, okay? Don't do anything else silly, you goose."

"I won't."

Antonia looked like she meant it, but Sophie had to be sure. "Pinky promise."

They hooked their little fingers together, and Antonia met her daughter's gaze gravely. "Pinky promise."

"Thank you. Bye, Mum."

Cooper struggled to breathe in the collared shirt he'd chosen to wear to dinner at his sister's. He hooked a finger into the collar and tugged it away from his skin, but it didn't help.

The truth of it was, the shirt wasn't strangling him; his nerves were. He'd never introduced a serious girlfriend to his parents. Plenty of the women he'd dated had tagged along to family dinner, but he hadn't cared whether his family approved of them. With Sophie, he feared that if his family—in particular, Aria—disapproved, she'd drop him faster than a hot potato.

One final inspection in the mirror, and he turned away.

"Hey, Soph," he called. "You ready to go?"

"Just a moment," she called from somewhere in the back of the house.

Cooper followed the sound of her voice to the bathroom and paused in the doorway, watching as she bent over to retrieve a hairpin from the floor. Her knee-length skirt drew tight across her ass and sent a bolt of desire straight to his groin.

Not a good time!

Discreetly, he adjusted himself and cleared his throat. Sophie jolted upright and swung around to face him as she stuck the pin into a messy bun on top of her head.

Her eyes narrowed. "Perv."

He grinned. "Just enjoying the view."

Mouth forming a reluctant smile, she cocked her hip to

the side, displaying her curves provocatively. "Let's forget about going out tonight. We could stay here and get to know each other even better."

Cooper's throat went dry. He stalked over and ran his hand down her hip and around her bum, grabbing a handful of hot flesh. He kept his gaze locked on her face, noticing the way her eyes darkened and her breath became thready. Her lips, painted a deep pink, parted, revealing the tip of her tongue. He kissed them, curling his other hand around her neck and stroking his thumb back and forth at the base of her hair. Her eyes fluttered closed, her eyelids shimmering with the makeup she'd applied, and her hands came to his hips.

With surprising strength, she dragged him against her. Cooper groaned as her body yielded, cradling his hard flesh. He had to end this before it got out of control. With a heavy sigh, he pushed away from her. Not an easy task when both she and his errant body wanted none of it.

"No," he said firmly. "We need to go tonight. I don't want to keep us a secret for any longer. Do you?"

"I suppose not," she replied unconvincingly. "But Aria is going to think I'm such a bad friend."

Cooper wanted to laugh to lighten the mood, but she'd struck a bit too close to the heart of his fears. "Don't worry, Shorty," he said, trying to keep his tone offhand. "She won't be mad at you. If she's going to be mad at anyone, it'll be me."

"Don't be silly." She rolled her eyes at him. "Everyone knows you can't help yourself. They'll probably think I'm using you as a rebound."

The thought gave him pause. "Are you?"

She shrugged. "Maybe at first, but not anymore. You're way more than a rebound hottie."

"Good." He knew he must look ridiculous, wearing a goofy, wide smile, but he didn't care. She made him happy.

He swept her into a hug, twirled her around and set her back on her feet. "How did I get so lucky?"

Sophie smiled lopsidedly. "It's a good thing I was so persistent, huh?"

"*You* were persistent?" he asked incredulously. "If I remember correctly, you were perfectly happy to move on to some other guy if I didn't take you up on your offer."

Good thing she hadn't, because he would have had to beat the crap out of any man who touched her. Even now, his fingers tightened around her waist at the thought of it.

"Was I?" she asked with a devilish wink.

His jaw dropped. "You *played* me?" Her smug expression was all the confirmation he needed. "I can't believe it!" he exclaimed, then paused. "Well, actually, I can. All I have to say is, well played, Shorty. You had me convinced."

"Thank you. Surely you can understand why." Standing on tiptoes, she pressed a conciliatory kiss to his cheek, then worked over to his lips and nibbled her way down the side of his neck to his chest. She purred low in her throat, and he clenched his teeth, determined not to start anything they wouldn't have time to finish. "All this chemistry," she continued, "and you were going to ignore it."

"It would've been the decent thing to do," he said.

"I didn't want decent. I wanted naughty."

He chuckled, and the sound came out sounding dirty. "Oh, baby. I can be naughty."

She grinned and stepped away. "I know you can. Now, go get the keys. We've got a dinner to get to."

Cooper swore. "You tease."

"You know it."

CHAPTER 15

They drove to Aria's together, ostensibly because it was more efficient. In reality, Sophie needed Cooper by her side, and she suspected he felt the same way.

After they parked, Sophie lingered at the roadside while he came around, then latched on to his hand. The sensation of their palms pressed against each other grounded her, and she took a deep breath, barely able to believe that she was about to charge inside and announce to her oldest friend that she was dating her brother.

What have you got yourself into, girl?

"You ready?" she asked Cooper in a whisper.

"As ready as I'll ever be," he replied.

"Come on, then." She tugged his hand, and together they walked up the short path to the cottage. A ginger cat lay sprawled on the couch next to the open door, and Sophie tickled his tummy as they walked past.

When they stepped into the kitchen, they were met by the usual chaos. Aria's hunky fiancée Eli glanced over his shoulder and smiled, then resumed stirring the contents of a wok on the stovetop. He swung around for a second look a moment later, his gaze dropping to their linked hands. Then he sidled over to Aria, who was cleaning salad greens in the sink, and murmured in her ear.

Aria spun on her heels and stared at Cooper and Sophie, eyes wide. One of her hands slapped up to cover her mouth, and she shrieked.

At once, everyone fell silent.

Donna and Geoff, Cooper's parents, stopped arguing over a spirited card game with Emily and Justin. Emily beamed. A scowl darkened Justin's face.

Aria raised a trembling hand and pointed. "You… Together… *What?*"

Sophie's heart seemed to have stopped beating. Her lips wouldn't move, rendering her incapable of replying. Luckily, Cooper didn't seem to be in the same predicament.

He squeezed her hand, waved with his other, and, the epitome of casual, said, "Hey, everyone."

Aria put her hands on her hips. "Explain yourselves."

For all that Sophie had thought she'd prepared for this, she felt her knees begin to buckle under the force of all the stares. Cooper released her hand, and his arm came around her waist to brace her. Thank God.

"Sophie and I would like you all to know that we're dating."

As Cooper's words penetrated the room, the silence grew even more fraught.

"So cute," Emily hissed to Justin, who quieted her with a look. For his part, he looked ready to strangle someone. Even though it was traitorous, Sophie hoped his anger was directed at Cooper rather than herself.

"Oh. My. God," Aria said, looking at a loss.

Eli wrapped his arms around her from behind. "What she means to say is, congratulations." His smile was warm, and relief flooded Sophie as she realized she had an ally.

"Thank you," she said, smiling back.

"We're very happy for you, darling," Donna said. "You took us by surprise, that's all. How did this come about?"

Sophie's cheeks heated. She couldn't very well tell them the whole truth. Bits and pieces of it, perhaps, but not the part where she'd propositioned Donna's youngest son.

"I couldn't say for Coop," she began, "but for me, it started a couple of weeks ago, when—"

"Sorry to interrupt," Justin broke in. "But can I speak to you outside for a moment, Coop?"

Without waiting for a reply, he rose from the table and stalked out. Sophie expected Cooper to make some pithy remark, but instead he followed Justin meekly from the room.

"Well, I never," Donna exclaimed, clearly gob-smacked. "I *know* I didn't raise that boy to be so rude." She reached over the table for the bottle of wine, poured a glass and pushed it towards the spot Justin had vacated. "Take a seat, honey, and tell us all about it."

After Sophie had sunk into the chair and sipped the wine, she laid her hands awkwardly on the table. Donna rested one of her hands over Sophie's.

"A couple of weeks ago, I broke up with Evan. I came over here to see Aria. She was away, but Coop was here." Sophie chuckled at the memory. "I jumped out from behind a bush and threatened him with a wine bottle. He took it pretty well, and it just kind of went from there."

"So *you're* the new girl." Aria clapped her hands excitedly. "The one who cured his nightmares."

"You knew he was seeing someone?" Geoff asked, speaking for the first time.

"Of course, he was seeing someone," Donna said, rolling her eyes. "That dear boy is always seeing someone. No offense, love," she added, patting Sophie's hand.

"But he said he was taking a break from women," Eli remarked, scratching his chin thoughtfully.

"I, um... I guess I ruined that," Sophie admitted. "Sorry."

"Oh, don't be sorry." Donna beamed at her. "I couldn't be more pleased to have you as part of the family. Although you know I've always thought of you that way. We're happy for you, dear," she said, casting a look at Geoff. "Aren't we?"

"Absolutely," he replied with conviction. "Cooper needs a steadying influence in his life, but I'm surprised he convinced you to give him a chance. I suppose you know he chronically avoids commitment?"

"Yes," she agreed wryly. "Up until now, apparently."

"He's also terrible at expressing his feelings," Aria commented.

Sophie recalled the way he'd knelt in front of her earlier and told her he wanted them to be more than a fling. "He's getting better at that."

Aria left Eli's arms and came over to hug Sophie. As she did, she murmured in Sophie's ear, "I'm really happy for you, Soph. Just be careful, okay? I don't want you to get hurt."

A lead weight dropped to the bottom of Sophie's stomach. It was yet another reminder that Cooper liked to play the field. Clearly, Aria was worried that he'd drop her once he became bored, just as Sophie herself had once believed. Hearing someone else voice her fear made it seem more real, but she shoved the thought to the back of her mind.

"I'll be careful," she promised.

~

"What your problem?" Cooper asked once he and Justin were out of earshot of the house.

"What's *my* problem?" Justin echoed disbelievingly. "What the hell is *your* problem?" He shoved Cooper's shoulder hard. "I honestly believed you when you said there was no girl this time. Stupid me, huh? But even though I know what you're like, I'm having a hard time believing you'd sink low enough to screw over Sophie. Really, man, have a little heart. She's way too sweet for your sick games. She's in a vulnerable place. Don't be the asshole who makes it worse."

"I won't make it worse," Cooper replied calmly, although the accusation stung. Especially from Justin, who was essentially his best mate. "I care about Sophie. She means a lot to me."

"Then do her a favor and stay the hell away from her."

Cooper shrugged. "I can't do that."

"The hell you can't. She doesn't deserve to have you run away from her in a few weeks once the novelty has worn off." Justin lowered his voice. "Do the right thing."

"Bro, I can't," Cooper said helplessly. He didn't care how selfish it was; he couldn't give up Sophie. She was different from the others. "We've got a really good thing going." Then inspiration struck. "What if she's my Emily?"

Justin's eyes narrowed. "What do you mean?"

"You were the mopey-est guy in Itirangi until Emily came along, and now look at you, practically radiating happiness." Okay, maybe that was an exaggeration, but it was true that Emily had made Justin a happier man. For God's sake, the moron was grinning just thinking about her. If that wasn't crazy, stupid love, Coop didn't know what was.

"I see your point," Justin allowed. "But I didn't date anyone for a year before Em. You've dated half-a-dozen girls in that time."

Cooper winced. Painted in that light, he sounded like a player. "How's this? If I mess up with Sophie, you can beat the shit out of me. Tag-team with Eli. You're both meatheads." Heck, if he hurt Sophie, he wouldn't fight back.

"You're serious about her?"

"I am. She's..." He struggled to think of the right words. "Amazing. Hot. Surprisingly strong. Did you know her mum has been bed-bound for two years, and Sophie's had to care for her?"

Justin nodded, and his shoulders relaxed. "I knew something wasn't right, but I didn't realize it was that serious."

A wave of shame washed through Cooper. Even hermit-like Justin had known more about Sophie's life than he had. "I didn't know anything about it," he admitted. "What does that say about me?"

Justin didn't reply. They both knew it wasn't good.

"I slept with her," Cooper added suddenly, startling even himself.

Justin rolled his eyes. "I could have guessed that."

"No, I mean I actually *slept* with her," he said meaningfully. "All night."

"Hmph," Justin grunted. The two of them didn't discuss feelings often, but surely he could see the significance of that. "Okay, I'm gonna give you the benefit of the doubt, bro, and assume you truly want the best for Sophie. But if you mess it up, you'd better be ready to deal with the consequences."

Cooper shook his brother's hand. "I won't mess it up."

He seemed to be making a lot of promises lately. He hoped he could keep them.

CHAPTER 16

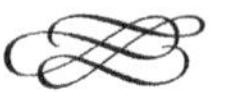

After several days of officially dating Sophie, Cooper wondered why he'd ever been afraid of being in a committed relationship. Waking up together, running together, sneaking in quickies between her appointments, falling asleep wrapped around each other's arms with no fear of nightmares—it was bliss. He couldn't fathom why Evan had been unfaithful to her. Who would care about the charms of any other woman when they already had a sweet, adventurous woman of their own? It boggled the mind.

Early Thursday afternoon, Cooper fixed himself a late lunch and ate it on his deck, enjoying the view of red and orange-hued trees. When he'd almost finished eating, he checked his watch. Sophie should have finished with her last client of the day. Hopefully, she'd be here soon. And hopefully, he could convince her to take off her tight little skirt, spread her creamy thighs and—

The doorbell rang. Cooper shot to his feet, stuffed the rest of his sandwich into his mouth, strode to the door, and yanked it open. "Great timing!" he exclaimed, only to see a face at the door that wasn't Sophie's.

Of course it isn't her, stupid. Sophie wouldn't knock.

"Glad to hear it," Midshipman Laura Dennis replied, sweeping a fall of long blonde hair over her shoulder. "Long time, no see, Coop. How're you doing?"

"L-Laura," he stuttered, then clamped his mouth shut once he realized it was hanging open. "What are you doing here?"

She shrugged, smiling up at him with deep brown eyes that crinkled at the corners, a result of her having spent months at sea. "I was in the area. Asked around and found out where you lived." She laughed. "Everyone really does know everyone around here. I always thought you were exaggerating."

"Nah." He shook his head ruefully. "Not exaggerating."

The familiarity of Itirangi didn't frustrate him as much as it used to, though. He'd come to appreciate the comforts of living in a small town. Less noise, fewer people. Less claustrophobic. "It's good to see you, Laura. Do you want to come in?"

"I'd love that." Her eyes crinkled again. "Damn, I could use a cold one."

"Coming right up."

Cooper stepped back to let her in, checking his watch again. His plans with Sophie were probably shot to hell now. He hadn't seen Laura in years, not since before the accident that had killed Ben and sent him home. No doubt she'd want to spend a while catching up.

"Kitchen is straight ahead," he said. "Help yourself to whatever you want from the fridge." Following her, he grabbed a beer for himself as well.

"Nice setup," Laura called. She'd let herself out onto the deck.

Cooper joined her and flopped into one of the seats. "How have you been?"

She didn't reply for a moment, just gazed out over his backyard and swigged the beer. "I get by."

He sighed, reading the subtext in what she'd said. She hadn't recovered any more than he had. "Same here. What do you do now?"

"I've been working as a private security consultant," she said. "Fancy name for a bodyguard. You?"

A lot of people would have been surprised to discover that the slender blonde protected people for a living. Not Cooper. Laura was a tough chick. Always had been.

"Wedding photography," he replied.

She snorted. "Cooper Simons, making a living by selling bullshit sentimentalist pictures. Never thought I'd see the day."

His hackles went up, but he consciously relaxed his shoulders. She meant nothing by it. "I enjoy it. It's nice to be in a job where people are happy to see me."

"Chill, Coop." She must have heard the defensive note in his voice. "Just a bit of ribbing between old friends. I'm glad you're doing something you like. If only all of us could be so lucky."

Her lips drew tight. For a moment, she looked as intense as she had all those years ago, preparing to enter a war zone. Then she shook herself, and the intensity vanished.

She smiled crookedly. "Anyway, I'll be around for a while. I've got a new client in the area. I thought of you and the good times we used to have."

Cooper remembered those days, too. They formed part of the adrenaline-fueled haze of his past. They'd been in a strange place and had found comfort in each other.

"Are you seeing anyone?" she asked.

He ran a hand through his hair and smiled. "Yeah, I am."

"Damn." One side of her mouth quirked down, but she didn't seem too upset. But then, it wasn't as if they'd ever really been in a relationship. They'd just been friends who occasionally relieved each other's sexual frustration. "Is it serious?" she asked.

He cocked his head. "More serious than I've ever been."

"What's she like?"

"Why do you want to know?"

She grinned. "I want to know what kind of girl convinced you to settle down. She must be something special."

"She is." He gulped his beer. "She's one of my sister's best friends."

"The sister who used to send the delicious baking?"

"Yeah."

For a moment, they both savored the memory of the packages Aria had sent to Cooper while he was stationed overseas. They'd been a highlight for many of the men and women in his squadron, some of whom never received so much as a letter from home.

"Does your girl cook as well as your sister?"

"Not at all." He chuckled. "Most of her meals come out of a box from the supermarket."

"Oh." Laura deflated. "That's disappointing. How about your sister? Is she single? Does she swing both ways? Because I'd love to meet the woman responsible for that fantastic cake."

Laura was open-minded about relationships, Coop remembered, with no preference for men or women.

"You're out of luck. Sorry. She's engaged, and several months pregnant."

"Any other sexy Simons siblings?"

"One." She started to talk, and he held up a finger to stop her. "Also not single."

She cursed. "Damn, you're a domestic bunch."

He supposed they were. The thought made him laugh. Who would have guessed it? Six months ago, he'd been a determined playboy, Aria was chronically single, and Justin was nursing a broken heart. How things had changed.

"I guess I'll have to find someone else to pass my time

with," Laura continued. "Or figure out what else there is to do in this place."

"I'll take you fishing sometime, if you like." He hadn't been out for a couple of weeks; he'd been too absorbed with Sophie. "There are some good rivers in the hills, and the lake is stocked, too."

"I might take you up on that. You got a boat?"

"My parents do."

At that moment, the door opened. Sophie was here.

SOPHIE FLOATED up the steps to Cooper's front door, lighter than air. She'd made the sale of the year this morning and had a big fat commission to show for it. On top of that, her mum had successfully checked into Trisha's care facility and had promised to cooperate with the doctors. So far, it had been a great day.

Sophie had bought a bottle of bubbly to celebrate with, and she was looking forward to indulging with Cooper. Along with the bubbly, a small package was clamped under her arm: a lace confection she knew Cooper would love taking off her. She hummed softly as she breezed through the door and headed straight for the deck. No doubt he'd devoured a sandwich and was growing grumpy waiting for her, but she could easily bring him around once he saw what she had in store for him.

As she reached the ranch slider, she glanced outside and froze with her hand on the handle.

Cooper was sitting out on the deck, his head bent in intimate discussion with a blonde woman.

Memories flooded back, visions of Evan with his blonde secretary while she stood in the doorway with a bottle of wine, unable to do anything but watch. She must have made a noise, because Cooper turned to look at her. Sophie backed away from the door, the package slipping from under her arm. He beckoned, but all she could do was gape.

Not again. Not with this man.

She stumbled back another few steps, then self-preservation kicked in and she wheeled and ran from the room. Her vision blurred with tears as she fled the house, and her heart spasmed as the heel of one of her shoes skittered over a pebble and her leg went forward while the other one flew out to the side. She skidded down the stairs, throwing her arms out to break her fall, but she landed hard on her hands and knees, losing both shoes in the process.

"Shit!"

Her wrist was throbbing, pain was screaming through her knees, and her palms were burning. She rolled onto her bum and stared at the tiny stones embedded in her skin, then glanced behind her. She didn't have time to dig them out, not if she wanted to escape before Cooper found her in a heap on the ground, her skirt streaked with dirt, her dignity in tatters.

The door began to open, and Sophie clambered to her feet and snatched up her shoes. Her bare feet pounded the pavement as she ran toward her car, and a tickle on her shin told her the scrape on one knee was bleeding, but she didn't stop. She lurched around to the driver's side of the car just as Cooper, with his long legs, caught up to her.

He grabbed her shoulder, and she shook him off.

"Don't touch me," she spat, spinning to glare at him. She would have preferred to flee, but if he forced a confrontation, she'd fight as viciously as a cornered cat. She was finished being weak.

He released her immediately. "What's wrong, Soph?" He looked down and noticed the cuts and scrapes on her legs and hands. "You're hurt."

He dropped to the ground and dabbed at her grazed knees with the bottom of his shirt. The open wounds stung, and Sophie jerked away, her breath hissing through her teeth.

"Don't," she said, putting her hands up to ward him off. "And don't play dumb. I saw you in there. With *her*." She injected her words with every drop of disgust she could muster for the latest in her string of cheating boyfriends.

Cooper straightened slowly, studying her as one might a crazed dog nipping at their ankles. "That's what this is about? You don't trust me?"

Behind the wariness, she caught a glimpse of hurt when the corners of his mouth turned down. He masked it quickly, making his expression impassive, but she felt a twinge of guilt anyway. Why should she, though? This was his fault.

"It's not a matter of trust. I *saw* you."

"You saw me catching up with an old friend."

"It sure didn't look like that was all it was."

He put his hands on his hips. "Laura was in the navy with me. I haven't seen her in years. She dropped by to say hi. *That's it.*"

Sophie didn't believe him. She couldn't. All right, so maybe she hadn't caught them red-handed, but something hadn't been right. "You're telling me that *Laura*"—she said the name like it was a dirty word—"has only ever been your friend? And that her visit is totally innocent?"

He hesitated. Only for a moment, but she saw it.

"You're being ridiculous," he said.

"Tell me," she demanded. "Tell me there's never been anything more than friendship between you." Her voice dropped a notch and turned pleading. "Tell me, Coop. I want to believe you."

His shoulders slumped. "We used to sleep together."

Sophie closed her eyes, unable to bear the sight of his gorgeous face. She could have sworn she heard something breaking, like shattered glass. Maybe that was her. It felt like her insides had collapsed and nothing was holding her together anymore.

"*Used* to," he repeated. "It was a long time ago. She thought I might like to rekindle the old flame, but I turned her down. I'd rather have you, Soph."

"You let her stay here even after you knew she was interested in you."

She loathed the whiny tone of her voice. She didn't want to be one of those women who were so insecure that they tried to control their men, but she couldn't seem to help it—a fact that only served to make her feel more pathetic.

"It's not like she was heartbroken. She hasn't been pining for me all these years. It was just physical between us."

Was she supposed to find that reassuring? Because she didn't.

"Look, I know I'm new at this relationship stuff," he plowed on, "but it seems to me like it won't work if you don't trust me." He reached out to caress her cheek, and she flinched. He snatched his hand away as if he'd been burned. "I can't be with someone who's always waiting for me to mess up. I know I've got a long way to go before I'm the man of anyone's dreams, but I'm trying. I really am."

"I know you are," she said, wishing she could erase the shadow behind his eyes. "And I'm sorry for being the way I am." Her voice caught on a sob. "I wish I was different. It's not your fault I'm screwed up." Another sob wracked her body, and her shoulders shuddered with the effort of containing a scream. "I'm sorry."

"Aw, come here, Shorty."

Cooper gathered her into his arms with such tenderness that the last of Sophie's defenses gave out and she started to bawl, her tears streaming down her cheeks and soaking into his shirt. She burrowed her face against his chest, horrified when her sobs became hiccups.

"I'm s-sorry," she hiccupped. "I'm such a mess."

"That's okay," he replied, stroking her back comfortingly. "It's not your fault. You just need to figure out whether you trust me. If you don't trust me, there's no point carrying on."

Even though it hurt, she knew he was right. She wanted to tell him that of course she trusted him, but the past five minutes served as evidence to the contrary.

"It's not exactly that I don't trust *you.* It's just that I don't know if I can trust *any* man." She might have imagined it, but she thought some of the tension eased from his shoulders, so she went on. "The thought of going through what I did with Evan all over again is unbearable."

"If I ever did that to you, I'd get the beating of my life from Justin."

She smiled reluctantly, although she noticed he hadn't promised he wouldn't do it. "Really?"

"Yeah. He told me to leave you alone. Said you were too sweet for me."

"Ha!" She barked out a laugh. "Little does he know."

"You *are* sweet. A little spicy, too."

Somehow, it felt like they weren't talking about her temper anymore. The change of topic helped her get some perspective, so she wiped her eyes on his shirt and shrugged out of his embrace, then stretched up to kiss his cheek affectionately.

"I'm sorry for overreacting and falling to pieces on you."

"I'm sorry, too. I didn't realize having Laura here would upset you so much."

Sophie stiffened at the mention of the other woman, recalling that she was waiting for Cooper inside, probably wondering what had happened to him. Her cheeks warmed with embarrassment. What must Laura think of her, running away like a schoolgirl? Likely that she had no spine, which wasn't far from the truth. On another day, she might have followed Cooper inside and made it clear to whom he belonged, but now her eyes were bloodshot, her nose was running, and her knees were scraped and bleeding. She looked a fright.

"I'm going to head home. You should go back inside and finish your visit."

"Come inside. I'll send her away."

His heart was in the right place, but she couldn't agree. "I can't, okay? Please don't push me."

His mouth formed an unhappy line. "Okay. But I want to know as soon as you decide where I figure into your life."

She nodded. "I'll let you know."

He bent over and kissed her mouth softly. "Don't forget how good things can be between us."

There was no need to be concerned about that. Sophie kissed him back and waved goodbye, reminding herself that it was only for a while.

CHAPTER 17

Another weekend, another wedding. Cooper snapped a candid picture of the happy couple as they mingled with their wedding guests on the lawn at Miller's Vineyard. The hardest part of his job was over, and the fun part had begun. Unfortunately, rather than absorbing the good vibes like he usually would, he was mulling over his woman problems. Since their argument two days ago, he hadn't heard from Sophie, and he didn't know where he stood with her. Had she decided she couldn't trust him, after all? Should he let her go? The prospect of a girlfriend who analyzed his every move was hardly appealing.

Cooper took another photo, focusing on the quiet groom rather than the vivacious bride. The groom was looking at his new wife with admiration written across his face. Cooper often left weddings with a reasonable idea of how long the marriage would last. He had a good feeling about this one.

A movement in the corner of his vision drew his attention to a man approaching him from the side, and he turned with a polite smile in place. When he saw who it was, the smile faded.

"Evan," he said curtly.

"Cooper."

Evan offered his hand, and Cooper shook it reluctantly. *Behave,* he told himself. *You have a professional reputation to uphold.* He nodded to the busty blonde woman on Evan's arm.

"This is Amber," Evan said. "Say hi, Amber."

Amber tossed her hair over her shoulder and appraised Cooper openly. "Hi," she murmured, her voice a warm invitation.

"Nice to meet you. You're Evan's girlfriend?"

Her upper lip stiffened, losing its sultry pout. "I guess you could say that."

"Speaking of girlfriends," Evan interjected, "I hear you're dating my little ex-baggage."

Cooper's insides turned to ice, and cold fury like liquid nitrogen bubbled just beneath the surface. "If you mean Sophie, then yes, I am."

Evan's forehead wrinkled. "I've got to ask, my friend: *Why*? Everyone knows you could sleep with any woman you want. Sophie's frigid. Worst shag of my life. Don't know what I was thinking, keeping her around for so long. And I'm sure that if she can't keep a guy like me entertained, then she can't keep someone like you entertained, either. So, what gives?"

Forget ice. The blood in Cooper's veins began to boil. A red haze descended over his vision as it became blatantly obvious why Sophie had such horrific trust issues. This man—no, he didn't deserve to be called a man—this *monster* had taken advantage of her generous nature and messed with her head. He was responsible for the self-doubt that plagued her. Cooper couldn't comprehend how anyone could do such a thing to another person.

Calmly, he set the camera aside. Then, before Evan could guess his intentions, he drew his fist back and launched it into Evan's face. It had been years since he'd served on active duty, but Cooper's arms were powerful from hours of weight training, and Evan dropped noiselessly to the ground.

Someone shouted. Amber's hand flew to her mouth.

Cooper stepped over Evan and said calmly, "First off, I'm not your friend. Secondly, I *love* Sophie, both in bed and out of it. Don't you dare speak about her that way again."

Lowering his fists, he backed away, allowing Amber to attend to her prick of a boyfriend. A muffled drone in the background grew to a roar as the wedding guests' furtive voices pierced the thick fog of his rage.

He slumped into a nearby seat. *Holy shit.* He'd fucked up now. He shook his head, his disgust turning inward. Cooper had punched a wedding guest. His business was screwed, he realized as he fisted and un-fisted his useless, no-good hands. It would take a significant lowering of his prices for him to have any hope of surviving the damage he'd caused tonight. Word would spread quickly. This was Itirangi, after all. He could only hope that the gossips would cut him a bit of slack because they all knew Evan was a douchebag.

And seriously, how could anyone be so fucking rude about Sophie? She was sassy, funny, strong. Perfect. He'd meant what he'd said in the heat of the moment. He loved her. Though he'd never consciously thought about it, and he didn't know when or how it had happened, somewhere along the way, he'd fallen for the pint-sized redhead. Now, he could only cross his fingers and hope she felt the same way.

He wasn't like Evan. He could wait forever and prove himself over and over again, if that was what he took. He needed to tell her that before she decided to ditch his worthless ass. Who cared if he walked out of the wedding at this point? He'd ruined it, anyway.

Cooper started to stand, but a hand on his shoulder shoved him back down.

"What the hell?" he demanded, looking up.

Sergeant Gareth Wayland towered over him, wearing a crisp uniform and a frown. "I could say the same to you."

"What's up, Gaz?" Cooper asked.

Gareth moved back a couple of steps so Cooper didn't have to crane his neck to look at him. The policeman scowled. "Anonymous caller rang the station and reported an assault. You hit someone, Coop?"

Cooper's stomach bottomed out. Yep, he was well and truly done for now. His being arrested would be the icing on the cake for the gossiping community. "I'll be damned. Someone reported me?"

"Of course they did. You can't go around assaulting people." Gareth sighed, running a hand through his close-cropped brown hair. "It's been years since this happened last. I thought you'd recovered."

Cooper looked away, embarrassed by the reminder of the last time he'd had a run-in with Gareth. A truck had backfired, and all of a sudden, he'd been back in Iran, attacking the nearest bystander. He was lucky not to have injured anyone, and equally lucky that the victim of that episode had been the understanding type.

"It's nothing like that, okay? Evan insulted Sophie."

Gareth nodded, and Cooper thought he saw a flash of understanding behind his cool eyes, but regardless, he brought forth a pair of handcuffs.

"Is it really necessary?"

"You assaulted someone," Gareth growled. "I can't just give you the evil eye and send you home. I have to see if he wants to press charges. In the meantime, you need to come downtown with me."

Cooper rubbed his eyes wearily. His declaration of love would have to wait.

~

Sophie had just read an email Antonia's new nurse had sent, complete with photos of Antonia in the garden at her temporary home. She typed a reply and attached a photo of herself with a big smile, then hit send.

The cottage seemed lonely without Antonia being only a short distance away in the Big House. While they didn't live together, Sophie had always known she was close. Not anymore.

The shrill ring of her phone cut through the silence, jarring her. She checked caller ID. Unknown.

"Hi," she said cheerfully. "Sophie, here. How can I help you?"

"Hey, Shorty. It's Coop." Her stomach turned upside down at the familiar timbre of his voice. "What are you doing at the moment?" he continued, blithely unaware of her rioting emotions. "Would you be able to come and pick me up?"

"Where from?" she asked, latching on to the second question. "Don't you have your own car?"

"Um, funny story, actually. I'm at the police station."

She gasped. "*What?*"

"It's not a big deal," he soothed. "Just come and get me. I'll explain everything."

Sophie glanced at her watch. Still early. The time seemed to pass more slowly when she was lonely. Cooper was giving her a reason to get out of the house, and he must have an interesting tale to tell. "I'll be there in five. Please tell me you're not in an orange jumpsuit."

"No jumpsuit," he confirmed. "Thanks, Soph."

"No problem," she said, feeling oddly flustered. "I'll be there soon."

She hung up, then dashed outside, hopped into her car and drove to the police station, which was located in a stout concrete building opposite the soccer field. She strode inside, heels clacking loudly on the tile floor.

Suzy, the receptionist, greeted her with a smile. "Well, if it isn't my favorite girl. How are you doing, honey? How's your mum?"

"I'm doing just great," Sophie replied. "Mum is okay, too." Not a total lie, for once. "How are you, Suzy?"

She hadn't seen the motherly receptionist more than a handful of times since her father had died. Sophie experienced a twinge of guilt. She should have made more of an effort to keep in touch.

"I'm ticking along," Suzy said. "Only another six months until retirement."

"Congratulations!" Sophie exclaimed. "If anyone deserves a break, it's you. Do you have plans?"

"Bill and I are going on a cruise." Suzy's smile was smug. "To celebrate freedom. After that, who knows what I'll do with myself."

"I'm sure you'll find a way to fill the time. Pick up a new hobby. Start working in the garden, maybe?"

"I always did fancy the idea of designing a rose garden," Suzy said thoughtfully.

"You should do it. Now, I'm here for Cooper Simons. Where can I find him?"

"Oh, you're here for *him.*" Suzy's forehead puckered. "I'd hoped you were here to see the sergeant."

"No, sorry." While Gareth was a good-looking man, he'd been hung up on Avery since forever. Sophie would never touch a man who wanted another woman. "So, where can I find Cooper?"

"He's in a cell out back. Let me call the sergeant for you." Suzy picked up the phone and hit a button.

"In a cell?" Sophie demanded. "What on earth is he in a cell for?"

"Assault," Gareth rumbled from the doorway.

Suzy lowered the phone.

"That's crazy!" Sophie protested. "Coop would never hurt

anyone."

Gareth's eyes widened, and he rocked back on his heels, surprised by her fervor.

"I mean," she continued more quietly, "not on purpose, anyway."

"Coop punched a man, Sophie. On purpose. Maybe he didn't think it through, but he did it. Luckily for him, no charges have been pressed, and no serious harm's been done."

Sophie's mind focused on the detail she noticed Gareth had excluded. "Who did Coop punch?"

He cringed ever so slightly. "Evan."

"Evan? My ex, Evan?" Cheating scumbag Evan.

"Yes, that Evan. They were at a wedding together. Coop was working. There was an altercation, and he struck Evan in the face."

Sophie crowed, "*Yes!*" and pumped her fist. "Go, Coop! Do you know why?"

"No." Gareth's frown deepened. "And I have to say, I don't approve of this bloodthirsty streak of yours. You shouldn't encourage him."

"I didn't. That is to say, I haven't. I've barely even mentioned Evan to Coop." Except for that first day. "And I can hardly believe Evan wouldn't press charges."

Gareth shrugged. "Guilty conscience?"

Doubtful. "Can I see Coop?"

"Yeah. Follow me."

Gareth twirled a keychain around one finger and turned on his heel, leading Sophie towards the back, where the overnight holding cells were located. He walked with a slight limp, the result of an old rugby injury.

"Can he leave?" she asked, trotting after Gareth.

"Yes, but I'd recommend you speak to him about that anger problem of his."

Sophie blinked, curious, then realized she'd stopped

walking and he'd left her behind. She hurried to catch up. "Anger problem? He doesn't have an anger problem."

"Sure seemed like it tonight."

They rounded a corner, and she spotted Cooper behind bars, leaning against the concrete wall, wearing a pair of dress trousers and a collared shirt and tie. He would have looked immaculate except that some of his hair had fallen loose and he hadn't bothered to fix it. For some reason, the imperfection made him appear disheveled and elevated him from merely sexy to mouth-wateringly hot.

Sophie wiped the edge of her bottom lip to make sure she wasn't drooling.

"Sophie." As soon as he set eyes on her, Cooper pushed off from the wall, rushed to the bars, and wrapped his fists around them.

Sophie stretched onto her toes to kiss him between the bars. "What happened?"

Cooper glanced at the sergeant, who was unlocking the bolted door, then focused on her, his intense grey-blue gaze skimming from her face down the length of her body and back up. "You look good." His voice was husky and low.

Sophie's lips quirked, and heat fizzed through her blood. "You're trying to distract me. Why'd you hit Evan? And tell me the truth. Don't gloss over it. I know what he can be like. It must have had something to do with me."

Scowling, Cooper shoved away from the bars and stalked through the door Gareth had unlocked. For a moment, she thought he wouldn't say more, but then he murmured to the sergeant, "Can you give us a moment, Gaz?"

Gareth hesitated.

"We won't make any trouble," Sophie added. "Promise."

"Okay," Gareth relented. "But if you're not out in two minutes, I'm coming back."

"Yeah, yeah." Cooper waved a hand dismissively.

"Thanks," Sophie said without looking away from her

lover. When Gareth was out of earshot, she crossed her arms over her chest. "So, what happened? Spill."

Cooper cupped her face, the gentle caress of his hands sending tendrils of pleasure tickling down her spine. "You're so gorgeous." He bent to kiss her, and Sophie melted against his burly chest, her arms coming undone and looping around him. "And strong, and special."

If he kept this up, her head would be so inflated, she wouldn't be able to fit back through the door. She returned his kiss softly until heat began to flare between them, then pulled back.

"Stop it," she chided. "Tell me what happened."

"Fine," he muttered. "Evan was being disrespectful towards you, so I straightened him out."

"Disrespectful how?"

"Just plain rude. It doesn't matter."

While she was intrigued to know what Evan had been saying to provoke Cooper into punching him, her gratitude that he was all right outweighed her need to know the truth. Besides, for him to have reacted in such a way, he must feel some deep emotion towards her.

"Come here," she said, and wrapped herself around him, resting her cheek over his heart, which was beating erratically. "Are you okay?"

"Yeah. I just..." His arm tightened around her. "Sophie, I need to tell you—"

"You've had your two minutes," Gareth interrupted from behind them. "Cooper, can I speak to you privately?"

Sophie released Cooper but didn't leave. His arm remained banded around her waist, and he wasn't giving any indication that he planned to let go either.

He lifted his chin. "Sophie can hear anything you have to say to me."

"If you insist." Gareth's foot tapped impatiently. "We've just got word that a murder suspect may be laying low in

Itirangi. Christchurch Police Department tracked him here using the GPS on his cell phone, but the phone died a few minutes ago. Either that, or he wised up and ditched it. The detective in charge of the operation has asked me to organize a manhunt. I'm short-staffed. You've got a military background. Can you lend a hand until support arrives?"

Cooper ran a hand through his hair. "Sure. What do you want me to do?"

"No!" Sophie screeched, her heart pounding so wildly in her chest that she could barely hear herself over its drumming. "You can't. It's too dangerous." She glared at Gareth. "He's not a policeman, and he's not in the military anymore. You have no right to ask anything of him." She rounded on Cooper. "And you—don't be stupid. It could be dangerous."

"It could be," Gareth acknowledged. "And you're right. I don't have any business asking Coop to help, but I'm asking anyway. As a friend." He held out a hand to Cooper. "You in?"

Cooper grabbed his hand and pumped it. "I'm in."

"Please don't," Sophie pleaded, desperate to break through the steely resolve she saw in Cooper's eyes and the set of his jaw. "Just take a second to think about it."

Cooper rubbed his thumb across her cheekbone. She wanted to squeeze her eyes shut and turn away, but she held his gaze, praying he could see how much she needed him to stay away from that murderous psychopath.

"There's nothing to think about," he said. "If there's anything I can do to keep Itirangi safe, to keep *you* safe, I have to do it."

Tears welled in her eyes, and she blinked rapidly to stop them from falling. She felt as though a fist had closed around her throat, and she struggled to breathe. *Keep composed,* she told herself. *Don't break down. Not here. Not now.*

She breathed in, counted to five, and breathed out again. Her lower lip trembled, and she bit it. Finally, she nodded, though it was more of a head-jerk, really.

"Go, then." Inwardly, she congratulated herself on sounding like she didn't care. True, her voice was harsher than the situation warranted, but some things couldn't be helped.

"I'll come back," he promised.

Sophie did look away now. "Don't make promises you can't keep."

Her father had promised he'd come home. Every morning, he'd kissed her cheek and said he'd see her in the evening. Then, one day, he hadn't, and she'd been left on her own, with a shell of a woman for a mother. Everything had gone to shit, and she wasn't about to watch history repeat itself.

"Text me afterward to let me know you're safe. But don't bother coming over."

Yanking out of his embrace, she stalked away, holding the tears at bay.

She drove home, changed into her pajamas, and turned on the TV. All the while, the great sucking hole inside of her grew larger. She wanted that big, stupid oaf to be safe.

More than that, she *needed* it.

CHAPTER 18

After staring at the TV for upwards of twenty minutes without really seeing anything and forcing herself to eat mac and cheese which had the texture of glue in her mouth, Sophie switched off the TV and gazed at her phone. She should call Cooper to make sure he was okay.

"Don't do it," she muttered to herself. "Don't be a doormat."

She should have learned not to care for men who recklessly threw themselves into danger, but she was her mother's daughter. Cletus leapt onto the couch next to her, and Sophie patted him distractedly, focused on Cooper's contact details on her screen. The phone vibrated in her hand, and she flinched in fright. Had she conjured him with her thoughts? Unfortunately not. The Caller ID showed it was Aria.

"Hey, Ri," she said when she'd recovered from her scare. "What's up, sweetie?"

"Turn on Rangi FM," Aria replied. "Now."

Without questioning her, Sophie flicked on the local radio station. "Done."

"Listen."

Sophie moved the phone away from her ear to give the radio her full attention. The news presenter was halfway through a sentence, but she caught the gist of it. They were reporting on a police chase in Itirangi. It seemed someone had caught up to the murderer.

"Witnesses report that a man, described as either a plain-clothes officer or a civilian, over six feet tall, blond and stocky, pursued the fugitive, who is wanted in relation to the murder of his girlfriend, into a private home at Raynor Street. The fugitive cornered his pursuer and stabbed him. The status of the victim is unknown at this time; however, the fugitive has been apprehended."

"Oh my God," Sophie gasped, the room seeming to spin wildly around her. "Coop?"

"That's what I was going to ask you," Aria said. "A friend called me just before this started to air. It sounds like him. But why would he be out chasing this guy?"

"Because Gareth asked him to," Sophie replied, clenching her fist so tightly that her nails cut into the palms of her hands. "I can't believe he'd be so stupid. I *knew* he'd get himself hurt. I need to get down there."

"Go. I'll be there as soon as I can."

She hung up and leapt from the couch, sweeping her keys from the coffee table on the way out of the house. Raynor Street wasn't far, and it would be faster to run than drive. Thankfully, running was something Sophie excelled at. She took off, her toned legs eating up the pavement, one phrase running through her mind like a mantra.

Let him be okay. Please, let him be okay.

Cooper came to with a start. He fought to sit up and instantly regretted it as a wave of nausea rolled through him and pain lanced up his shoulder like he'd been jabbed with a hot poker. Cringing, he dropped back onto an uncomfortable surface. Not a bed—too hard and unyielding for that—but not the ground, either. His neck jarred painfully when it fell farther than the rest of his body.

"Ouch."

"You're not swearing," an amused voice said from somewhere near his head. "That's a good sign."

Cooper tried to find the source of the voice, but his vision was foggy, and every time he tried to focus, patches of light danced across his view. "What happened?" he tried to ask, except it came out sounding more like "Wha' hap'n'd?"

A silhouette appeared above him. "Do you know what day it is?"

What the hell did it matter? His annoyance must have registered on his face, because the man added, "Bear with me."

"Saturday."

"Good, good. What do you last remember?"

He thought back. He'd been working at a wedding, then he'd punched someone. He recalled being taken to the police station, reuniting with Sophie, and the disappointment on her face as he agreed to something that she didn't want him to do. He tried harder to remember what they'd argued about.

"Being at the police station," he said slowly. "I was helping Gaz out with something."

"Good," the man said again. "That was only a couple of hours ago. You're doing well."

"What happened?" Cooper asked, more clearly this time.

"You joined a search for a fugitive. You followed him into a house." The man waved toward a particular house, but since Cooper's sight was blurry, he couldn't see anything. "When you caught up to him, he stabbed you through the shoulder with a hunting knife."

"Stabbed?" That explained the burning sensation in his

shoulder. As if he didn't have enough scars already. Sophie would kill him. *If* she deigned to speak to him.

"Yes," the man—a paramedic, he assumed—said patiently. "Lucky for you, it missed all the major arteries. I've stitched you up. You were bleeding heavily, and I didn't want to risk further blood loss by delaying until we reached the hospital."

"Where are we?" Cooper's vision was clearing, but not enough for him to ascertain where they were.

"You're in an ambulance, parked on Raynor Street. You remember where that is?"

Cooper nodded, and a sharp pain flared through his temple. "Damn."

"Ah, yes," the paramedic said knowingly. "After you were stabbed, you fell and hit your head. You have a nasty bump, and most likely a mild concussion. We'll take you to the hospital for observation overnight. Unless anything worsens, you'll be released tomorrow, but it would be best if someone could keep an eye on you for the next few days. Is there someone you can stay with?"

Cooper started to nod, thought better of it, and said, "Yes," instead. "So long as she forgives me." He could tolerate Sophie seeing him in his weakened state, but no way in hell would he let his parents see him like this.

"Problems with the missus? Nothing I can help you with there."

He sighed. "You sure there's nothing you can prescribe?"

"I'm not a doctor, let alone an expert on affairs of the heart, but a good dose of groveling usually does the trick. Now, I'm going to crank you into an upright position. Is that okay?"

"Go for it."

The paramedic set to work. Cooper's vision cleared, and slowly the sea of faces outside came into view, as well as the frontage on the other side of the road, where a news van was parked. The paramedic rounded the stretcher, and Cooper could see what he couldn't before: that the man was young, not much more than twenty.

"Are you sure you know what you're doing?" he asked, even though he had no reason to believe the medic to be less than competent.

"Of course I do." The younger man was completely unphased by the question. Likely, he was asked several times a day. "Now that you're upright, it's nice to meet you properly. I'm Manaia."

"Cooper."

"Yes, I know." Manaia grinned. "You're a bit of a hero at the moment. How are you feeling?"

"Like I was stabbed by a madman."

"Good."

"Excuse me?"

Manaia shrugged. "Maybe you won't be so eager to run into danger next time."

Cooper huffed a half-hearted laugh. "Did Sophie put you up to this?" The confusion in Manaia's eyes was answer enough. "Never mind."

"There's a woman outside asking after you. She says she's a friend of your sister's. Would you like me to let her in?"

Sophie. She'd come for him. Cooper breathed a dizzying sigh of relief. "Yes, please."

But the woman Manaia showed into the ambulance wasn't Sophie. In fact, Cooper wasn't sure he'd ever met her in his life. He couldn't be certain; he was acquainted with many women, but he liked to think he could recognize one of Aria's friends. This woman—a tall, slim, brunette with intelligent brown eyes and a notepad tucked under her arm—didn't jog any memories.

"I don't know you," he said bluntly.

The brunette smiled. Not an ex-lover, then. "I'm Nina. I work with Aria at the newspaper."

A colleague, not a friend.

"I thought you were someone else." The only person he wanted to see was Sophie. He looked to Manaia, wishing the paramedic would send her away. No such luck. He seemed to be enjoying the show. Sadistic bastard.

"That's fine." Nina brought the notepad out from under her arm. "I've just got a few questions for you, and then I'll be on my way."

"I've been stabbed," he reminded her. "Surely the inquisition can wait."

"You said you were up to visitors," she replied, neatly turning the tables.

"That's when I thought you were—"

"Someone else," she finished for him. "Yes, I know. Who did you think I was? That would be a good starting point."

"Why?"

Her eyes widened. "You didn't catch Mr. Watters, but you're the hero of the day. Well, one of them," she amended. "I still need to speak to Ms. Dennis, since she incapacitated Mr. Watters after he stabbed you, but she wasn't heroically injured, so she can wait." Nina flipped her hair. "Cooper, people will want to know what you were thinking when you ran into that house and who you thought of when you realized you weren't going to die."

Cooper's temper began to rise, but he tried to tamp it down. This woman had a flair for the dramatic, and his supply of patience had dwindled perilously low. "Jesus, it wasn't that dire. I don't know why everyone is acting like I'm either an idiot or Superman. It was no big deal."

Well, he *had* been stabbed. But still.

"Cooper," Nina said, leaning closer. "Can I call you that?"

"I guess so," he grumbled.

"Cooper, you chased Mr. Watters. That was very brave."

At that moment, the ambulance door flew open again and Sophie hurled herself inside the ambulance—which was rapidly becoming cramped. She was wearing striped flannel pajamas, and her hair was in disarray. He'd never been more pleased to see anyone.

"Coop!" she exclaimed. "You're okay!"

"Of course I'm okay," he replied. "I don't know why everyone is making a big deal of this."

Sophie grinned so widely that he worried her face might split. She looked as though she might plant a sloppy kiss on him, which he'd have no problem with.

Then she caught sight of the reporter, and her grin morphed to a dark scowl. "Who are you?"

"Nina."

The reporter offered a hand, which Sophie ignored, moving instead to Cooper's side to place a gentle kiss on his cheek. Not quite the smooch he'd wanted, but he'd take what he could get at this stage. He was surprised to find that her territorial behavior stirred a flair of excitement in him. It meant she wanted him, and that she wasn't going to run this time just because of some perceived competition.

Sophie's eyes flicked to the notepad. "You're a reporter?"

"That's right. I was just telling your boyfriend how brave he was today. I need to ask a few more questions, and then I'll be on my way."

Cooper gave Nina credit. She didn't back down when faced with a fuming woman.

Sophie folded her arms crossly. "There will be no questions. Can't you see he's been hurt? Give him some time to recover, for pity's sake."

"I'll be as unobtrusive as possible." Nina had a determined gleam in her eye. "I'll be gone before you know it."

"No," Sophie replied firmly. "Not now. If you want your story, go talk to someone else or wait until tomorrow."

"Okay, I understand." Nina slipped the notepad into her shirt pocket and handed Cooper a business card. "Give me a call when you're feeling better."

After she'd left, Manaia chuckled awkwardly. "Well, that was tense."

Sophie and Cooper both ignored him.

"Thank you," Cooper said as Sophie turned to him and exclaimed, "You were *stabbed*?"

"It's a flesh wound. Right, Doc?"

"A large flesh wound, yes," Manaia confirmed, not helping at all.

"You're so stupid!" Sophie yelled. "Why would you think it was a good idea to chase a murderer? Huh?" Before he had a chance to reply, she continued, "I know you have a case of survivor's guilt, but that doesn't mean you should risk your neck without thinking about anyone else. What would your parents have done if you'd been killed? Did you think about that? They love you. Do you know how relieved they were when you came back from the war? They deserve better than to have you running around like some headless chicken, practically inviting a bad guy to have a go at you. What would your family have done if he'd stabbed you a few inches across?"

He honestly hadn't given it much thought. Now that he had, the pain in his shoulder no longer bothered him as much as the guilt that sat heavily in the bottom of his stomach. Had he really worried his parents that much? Had he, in trying to do the right thing, hurt the people he loved?

"I'm sorry," he offered.

Sophie took a deep breath, and it saddened him to see the tears gleaming in her eyes. "Sorry won't cut it. Do you know how *I* would have felt if you didn't come home? I was so—" She stopped herself from saying whatever words were about to spill from her lips and began again. "And then I come here and find you chatting with some reporter. Do you realize how that makes me feel?"

Angry would be his best guess.

"I care about you, Coop." Her chin wobbled. "But you're not making it easy."

He reached for her, but the burning sensation in his shoulder shot down his arm, and he retracted it. "I'm sorry," he said again, feeling useless. "But it's who I am. I can't help it, and I'm too tired to argue with you right now. Do you think you could give me a break?"

"Sure," she replied all too easily, then turned to Manaia. "He'll be okay?"

"No doubt about it."

"Then I'll see you later, Coop." She kissed him chastely. "Make sure you look after yourself."

He should have asked her to wait, but he didn't know what more he could say to erase the wariness from her face. To erase the doubt. He was sick and tired of her doubt, so he let her go.

Manaia whistled. "That's quite a woman. You may need more than groveling."

Cooper grunted in agreement. "Yeah, I don't think groveling will be enough this time."

And unfortunately, he didn't know what else he could do.

CHAPTER 19

"You don't need to fuss over me," Cooper said for the tenth time as Aria plumped the cushion behind him and Donna placed a plate of chocolate chip cookies, fresh from the oven, on his lap. "On second thought..."

Donna grinned. "I thought that might change your mind. The way to a man's heart *is* through his stomach."

"Are these all for me?" Cooper asked as he munched on one, savoring the gooey melted chocolate.

"That plate is," Donna said. "The rest are for your sister. If you get between a pregnant lady and what she's craving, you might lose an arm."

"You reckon?" He eyed the plate of cookies on the table, which Aria was digging into.

She twisted around and glared at him. "Don't even think about it."

"Okay." He held his right hand up to fend her off. "I won't."

Geoff's laughter boomed from the couch on the other side of the room. "Accept it, son. The women are in charge in this family."

"And I wouldn't have it any other way," Cooper replied, afraid his mother might decide to confiscate the cookies if he answered differently. "You know, you don't all need to babysit me. It's only a wounded shoulder. I've had worse. I'll be fine."

Their expressions darkened. In moments like this, Cooper always wished he had a camera to snap a photo and show Aria how much she resembled Donna.

"We know you've had worse," Aria said. "But we weren't there to see it, and we'd rather not think about it." She slipped an arm around their mother's shoulders protectively, as if she were the one who needed comforting, rather than Cooper, who'd been stabbed and then deserted by the woman he loved.

Sophie's words from yesterday played through his mind: *What would your parents have done if you'd been killed? Did you think about that?* Cooper studied Donna's face, stripped of color, and glanced over at Geoff, who looked older than his sixty years. Had he taken his family for granted this whole time?

"I love you all," he told them. "You know that, right?"

Donna smiled tentatively, Aria's gaze softened, and Geoff—never one to discuss feelings—cleared his throat.

"Oh, honey," Donna said, coming over to gather him in a gentle hug. "Of course we do. And we love you. That's why we all wish we could have done more to help you when you came back. But you had to figure things out for yourself."

He remembered those first few months after Ben's death. He'd felt terrible for surviving when his best friend—a partner and father—hadn't. While Cooper had been thrilled to see his family, he'd also been riddled with guilt because Ben would never see his family again, so he'd pushed them away. It had taken a lot of therapy and time alone before he'd accepted the way things had turned out. He'd never escaped the subconscious guilt, though. The dreams had haunted him. Until Sophie came along.

"I wish it could have gone differently," he said.

"So do we." Aria said sympathetically. "But you can't change the past."

He inclined his head in acknowledgment. "If wishes were horses, huh?" He paused. "That's a stupid saying. Where does it even come from?"

Aria opened her mouth as if to explain. He glared at her, not really wanting a lesson on old British proverbs. She closed her mouth. No one said a word. He sighed.

"Sophie told me off. Said I was being reckless. I think she was really mad. I'm not too sure why, or how I'm supposed to fix it."

Geoff turned up the volume on the TV. No surprise there. Cooper looked to Aria just in time to catch her rolling her eyes.

"What is it?" he demanded.

She swatted his arm—the uninjured one, thank God. "You are *so* thick. Sophie was worried sick about you."

"She was?"

"Absolutely! When she found out you'd been hurt, she ran straight over to find you."

The thought of Sophie panicked about his welfare pleased him, although the pleasure was accompanied by a pinch of guilt. "She yelled at me."

"Because she was frightened stiff, idiot."

"It wasn't that big of a deal." A line he'd repeated a dozen times.

Aria looked meaningfully at his freshly dressed stab wound. "My guess is, it would be a big deal to someone who lost her dad in the line of duty."

Of course. Finally, everything clicked into place. They'd been so young when it happened that he sometimes forgot

Sophie's father, Mike, had died in a car crash during a high-speed police chase.

He cursed. "No wonder she didn't want me joining the manhunt."

"It probably felt a little too much like the past repeating itself," Donna said. "The poor dear is terrified of losing the men in her life. You saw how hard she clung to Evan, who clearly wasn't worth her time."

"You think that's because of what happened to Mike?"

"I think," Donna began, selecting her words carefully, "that Evan would never have lasted as long if Mike were alive."

Cooper frowned. "Hang on a minute. If she's afraid of losing me, then how come she left? It seemed more like she was angry."

Aria huffed in annoyance. "There's no point asking Mum and me these questions. We can only guess. Why don't you go ask Sophie?"

"Because she doesn't want to see me."

Donna smirked. "You've gotten lazy." She raised an eyebrow knowingly at Aria. "He's not used to having to work to win a woman over."

"I win women over all the time," he protested.

"Yes," Donna agreed. "With minimum effort, and as soon as they want more, you run for it." When he made a noise of disagreement, she shushed him. "I love you, but if you want a woman like Sophie Delaware, you have to be willing to compromise sometimes." She came over and patted his cheek. "You're a charmer, Cooper. Go show Sophie how charming you can be."

"I will." He stood, ignoring the way his head spun and his vision blurred. "Can you drive me, Ri?"

"Sure." She steadied him, and they left the house.

Cooper smiled to himself. Only a couple of months ago,

he'd helped Aria get the man of her dreams. Hopefully, she could return the favor.

~

Sophie didn't care that half the world had seen her in her pajamas, or that she'd been mentioned on the front page of today's newspaper. That paled in comparison to the fact Cooper had been stabbed, and he hadn't seemed even remotely concerned.

She poured herself a glass of wine with shaky hands, replaying everything that had happened yesterday for the millionth time. Then she grabbed a fistful of Doritos and savored the crunchy texture in her mouth. Chasing the Doritos down with a slurp of wine, she leaned against the kitchen counter, petting Cletus, who'd taken up residence on a pile of newspapers. She didn't have the heart to scold him for being on the counter.

Closing her eyes, she recalled the scent of disinfectant in the ambulance, the cloying warmth and the stale air. The panic that had surged through her veins, propelling her forward when she saw the bandage over Cooper's wound and realized he could have died. Then where would she have been? She couldn't lose the man she—no, she wouldn't even think the word. She couldn't feel that way about him. Not after a couple of weeks.

But you've known him your whole life.

She ignored the voice in her head. She'd never really known Cooper, not until now, just as he'd never really known her. Maybe if they'd gotten together years ago, he wouldn't have gone away to war and ended up with a guilt complex. But then he wouldn't have become the man she loved, either.

There, she'd admitted it. She loved him. She didn't want to. Loving Cooper could end poorly—but Sophie would protect herself. She was beginning to realize she was stronger than she'd ever given herself credit for.

"Screw him." She downed the rest of her wine, feeling it burn the back of her throat.

She needed a friend. Not Aria; that would be awkward. Avery's tough love would be better. Avery had gotten her through the situation with Evan only a few weeks ago. She could sure as hell tell Sophie to toughen up now.

She called.

"Hey," Avery answered. "I heard about what happened. How's Coop?"

"Okay, I think," Sophie replied. Tears threatened, making her tongue seem thick as she tried to shape it around some words. "Can you tell me to toughen up?"

Avery didn't hesitate. "Take a concrete pill and harden up, Soph."

Sophie smiled tremulously. "You're the best."

Avery snorted. "Of course I am. What's this about?"

But Sophie didn't answer, because she heard the click of the front door opening and heavy steps rushing up the hall. She knew the sound of those footfalls, since they'd come up the hall a number of times over the past few weeks. But what was Cooper doing here when he should be at home, being pampered by his parents?

She walked towards the hall as Cooper shoved the door open with his good arm.

"What are you—?"

She didn't get a chance to finish, because his lips covered hers and his arm came around her, his hand splaying across her lower back and pressing her closer to him. She should have resisted, but his kiss was too sweet, and the press of his hard chest and the possessive way his hand rested on her back were too tempting.

She ended the call and dropped the phone. Heat pooled in

her belly, and she kissed him back, winding her arms around his neck, careful not to bump his shoulder.

The kiss went on, neither of them willing to break it. Finally, she pulled away to catch her breath, resting her face in the crook of his neck and panting. The rapid rise and fall of his shoulders told her he was as breathless as she.

"What was that?" she asked when she had enough presence of mind to string together a sentence.

"I was an idiot," he puffed, his chin digging into the top of her head.

"Yeah, you were," she agreed, feeling somewhat mollified.

"I didn't see how scared you were," he continued, stepping back to meet her gaze. Sophie stared into his beautiful blue eyes, wishing she could interpret the pool of emotion swirling in them. "No wonder you were upset, considering how you lost your father. I didn't realize you cared about me enough to be scared."

"Petrified," Sophie corrected him, her tongue thick again. "I can't lose another man I care about like that. Do you know what it would do to me?"

His gaze softened, and he took her hand, his thumb sweeping gently over her knuckles. "You're stronger than you think, Soph. You could get through anything."

He'd echoed her earlier thoughts. She turned away, breaking eye contact. "That's not the point."

"Hey, look at me," he said, but she ignored him. "Come on, look at me. Hey. I know you, Sophie Delaware, and I'm telling you that you're much stronger than you could even imagine."

"So? Maybe I could handle losing you, but I don't want to. It would hurt, Coop. Even worrying about you hurt."

"I'll do my best not to worry you like that again. I promise."

"Haven't I already asked you not to make promises you can't keep?"

Cooper let her hand go and lifted her chin, forcing her to look at him. "What if I promise not to pull another stupid stunt unless I have your approval?"

She scoffed. "You love danger. You can't help it."

"Maybe. But I'll do whatever it takes if it means I get to come home to you. I'm not going to lie; I don't know much about love, but I think I'm in love with you."

Sophie gasped. "You what?" She studied his face for any sign of uncertainty and found none. "I think I love you too."

"Oh, thank God." He exhaled roughly. "In that case, I don't just think I love you. I know I do." She cocked her head quizzically, and he admitted, "I didn't want to scare you away. I love you, Sophie. I'm sorry for being an idiot. Please say you want me in your life."

"I do." The words came out softly, so she repeated them more firmly. "I do. But no more feeling guilty for being alive, okay? Because if you weren't alive, then I'd never have gotten the chance to be with you, and I'm so grateful you're the one who came back from the war."

"So am I," he said for the first time. "No more guilt. Cross my heart."

"Good." She smiled smugly. "Say the 'L' word again."

"I love you," he said, grinning. "You're so lovable, Shorty."

She laughed. "So are you. Now, shut up and kiss me."

EPILOGUE

CHRISTMAS, LATER THAT YEAR

"Isn't she precious? She's going to be a real looker one day." Cooper smiled fondly at his niece, crossed his eyes until she laughed, then handed her back to Aria, who kissed the top of her daughter's head.

"My little Laurie-the-looker."

Elijah wrapped an arm around Aria, and Cooper retreated, not wanting to intrude on their private moment when he'd much prefer to find Sophie and have a private moment of their own. Looking across the room, he caught sight of Antonia propped on the couch beside Donna and winked at her. Then he went looking for the love of his life.

He found her sitting on the deck, which had been bedazzled with flashing green and red lights, chatting with Avery.

"Hey, lover," he said by way of greeting, and was pleased when her cheeks flushed pink and the blush spread beguilingly down her neck.

"You're shameless," she said, laughter in her voice.

Cooper winked at Avery. "Can I steal Sophie away from you? I promise my intentions are anything but honorable."

Avery's lips twisted in a smirk. "Go ahead." She waved a

hand flippantly. “If anyone deserves a good roll in the hay, it’s Soph.”

“You’ll get no arguments from me.” Taking the hand Sophie offered, he pulled her out of the chair, and they strolled together down the back of the yard amongst the trees.

“Do you know,” she said thoughtfully, “it was about eight months ago when you nearly made love to me against a tree.” Her brow crinkled, and she somehow managed to look entirely innocent as she ran a hand down his front, pausing at the top of his jeans. “Remind me why you stopped?”

He made a choked sound. Even after months of dating, a single touch from her inflamed him. “Some misplaced idea about respect, I think.”

Sophie flicked the zip of his jeans open and hummed her appreciation. “You don’t still have those misplaced ideas, do you?”

“Um…” Distracted by the fact that she’d stripped off her top, he could barely think, let alone reply.

“Didn’t think so.”

As she yanked up her skirt, a smile caught his lips. “God, I love you.”

Her smile turned impish. “I know.”

“You know?” he asked, feigning surprise. “Are you sure?”

“Yes,” she confirmed, then leapt up and wrapped her legs around his waist, and he thanked his lucky stars he was quick enough to catch her. “But you’re welcome to show me.”

He grinned. “You know what? I think I will.”

THE END

IT WAS ALWAYS YOU - EXCERPT

Sergeant Gareth Wayland slowed his police cruiser to a stop beside the picnic area adjoining Lake Itirangi, an expanse of glacial blue water that formed the boundary of the township by the same name. It translated to "Little Sky" in Te Reo, the language of New Zealand's Maori people. He wound down the window and leaned out.

"Mrs. Dodds," he called. The frail white-haired lady trying to coax her feisty feline Milo down from a tree didn't turn. "Mrs. Dodds!" he called again, more loudly.

She looked over her shoulder, then smiled. "Sergeant," she said. "How lovely. You have the best timing. Do you think you could rescue my Milo for me? He's gotten stuck again, and I do worry he might fall and hurt himself. He's terrified, poor dear."

Gareth wondered if Mrs. Dodds' vision was failing as well as her hearing. Milo was decidedly *not* terrified. The ginger tomcat hissed and spat as though he'd gladly tear Gareth limb from limb. But Mrs. Dodds tilted her face up hopefully and the thick glasses that sat askew on her nose magnified her pleading eyes to twice their normal size. He sighed. Once again, he'd be going up a tree after her damn cat.

"Sure thing, Mrs. Dodds," he said, getting out of the car and taking a deep breath to fortify himself. Being a cop in a small town meant, first and foremost, taking the residents' problems seriously. "I'll have Milo down in just a moment."

Wrapping his palm around a branch above his head, he hefted himself up the trunk and wedged his foot into the split between the trunk and the first branch. Slowly, he ascended another two branches, arriving at the one Milo clung to. His left foot slipped and a nerve twinged in his bad knee. He grimaced.

You knew this was going to happen, he reminded himself. *As soon as you stopped the car, you knew you'd end up here.*

And yet, there he was. Like a masochist. Or the lone policeman of a practically crime-free town, whom the locals viewed as their personal errand boy. Tugging the ends of his uniform shirt over his palms to protect them as much as possible from Milo's claws, Gareth inched along the branch and reached for the cat, who yowled the instant they touched.

"Be careful with him," Mrs. Dodds called, her voice warbling. "He's very fragile."

He studied the furious kitty, with his fluffy coat and squishy belly. "Fragile, my ass," he muttered. Then he grabbed the cat.

Though he expected it, nothing could have prepared him for the pain of four sharply-clawed feet digging into his arms as Milo struggled to break free. He switched hands, holding Milo up by the scruff of his neck, and the cat quieted. *That's more like it.* It had taken a year to learn this trick. Twelve months, during which he'd spilled more blood than he rightly should have.

Holding the cat far away from his body, Gareth backtracked down the tree and jumped, landing on the ground with a thud, the vibrations causing a dull ache in his left knee.

"Here you are," he said to Mrs. Dodds, handing the hateful creature over. "Safe and sound."

Of course, Milo immediately curled into her arms and purred happily. Little demon.

"Thank you, dear," she replied. "You know how much I appreciate it." She smoothed a hand over the cat's head and ruffled his fur. "Say, my great-niece is visiting this weekend. Lovely girl. Wish I saw her more often. Why don't you come and have dinner with us?"

"Gee, thanks for the offer," Gareth began, "but I'm on duty this weekend." He shrugged as if to say, "what can you do?". "Someone needs to keep this place safe."

Her lips firmed into a line. "Oh, but can't someone else cover your shift for just one night? I promise you'll like my Camille."

He shook his head sorrowfully. "Afraid they can't, Mrs. Dodds. I'm sure I'll be able to meet Camille some other time." He tipped his hat to her. "You have a good day, now."

Spinning on his heel, he strode back to the cruiser. He had, in fact, met Camille Dodds before, and she was a lovely girl. Lovely, but not for him. Just like all of the other pretty young relatives the local biddies tried to set him up with. The fact was, he was happy single. Or if not happy, then at least, not unhappy.

Static crackled on his radio and he paused to listen.

"Attention all. A break-in has been reported at Sandiford's Laboratory on Walsh Street. Nothing missing so far, but part of the property has been vandalized. Unit seven, please respond. Repeat, unit seven, please report to the site immediately."

Gareth frowned. Sandiford's Laboratory was where his ex-girlfriend, Avery Brown, worked.

Avery.

Even thinking her name brought a wave of complicated emotions washing over him. Tenderness and concern, because she was the only girl he'd ever connected with on a soul-deep level. Confusion and frustration, because he'd always thought they'd reunite one day, but she treated him as nothing more than a distant acquaintance.

The call repeated. Unit seven being requested to cease any other activities and respond immediately. Interesting. Unit seven was the highest ranked unit in the district and boasted a pair of top-notch cops, one of whom was forensically trained. Their being assigned made no sense, in the circumstances. Why would two highly decorated officers be sent to handle a simple case of breaking, entering, and vandalism?

Unless it wasn't so simple.

Against his better judgment, he found himself doing a U-turn and heading toward Sandiford's Laboratory. He wasn't nearby, but if Avery was in trouble, he needed to be there. Switching the sirens on, he increased speed and raced toward the nearby town of Timaru, and Avery.

When he arrived, unit seven were already on the scene. He parked outside and hurried into the building, flashing his badge to the recruit on the door. He entered a long corridor with clinically white walls and sighted a uniformed officer at the far end. The officer stood beside a door that was ajar. Even from a distance, he could see that the laboratory had been trashed. Someone had done a number on it with a blunt object and a whole lot of rage.

Senior Constable Nathan Lang hovered inside, wearing his usual unflappable expression, but Gareth spotted something different in his eyes. Something fascinating. *Nerves.* But why would a veteran officer be nervous?

As he passed through the doorway, he began to understand. Facing Lang, hands balled in fists at her sides, jaw clenched, speaking through gritted teeth, was his high school sweetheart.

Yeah, so maybe "sweetheart" wasn't the right word. She was a dynamo.

"I know you have an investigation to complete," Avery Brown ground out, oblivious to his presence. "All I'm saying is, perhaps you could be a little more careful around my terribly expensive, world-class equipment."

"With all due respect, ma'am—"

"Ma'am?" she interrupted, clearly mad enough to spit tacks, her blue eyes like icy beams of fury. "Ma'am? I'm a doctor. I call you by your title, because I know how hard you worked to earn it, and I'd appreciate it if you did the same."

Lang glanced up at the roof, his lips moving silently as though whispering a prayer for patience. "My apologies, *Doctor*," he said, and though Avery had pushed his buttons, Gareth could tell she'd also earned his grudging respect. "But as you can see, your world-class equipment is already damaged beyond repair."

His tone wasn't unsympathetic, but Avery's laser-beam eyes narrowed. "Don't make anything worse," she snapped. "Your partner over there," she gestured vaguely behind herself, "is competent. How about you leave handling the equipment to him?"

Lang nodded shortly. "I can do that, ma'am—uh, Doctor."

Finally, her gaze ventured away from Lang's face and swept to the side, focusing on Gareth. As usual, she momentarily stole his ability to speak. Even dressed in a full-body suit with her long brown hair tucked inside a hairnet, she was stunning. Though that couldn't be attributed only to the way she looked, but also to the gleam of intelligence in her eyes and the way she held herself like she'd never experienced a moment of self-doubt in her life.

"Sergeant Wayland," she said, crossing her arms over her chest, her expression going from cold to downright arctic. He didn't like it, the way she tended to clam up around him. He had no clue why she felt the need to.

"Wayland," Lang said with a nod.

"Lang," he replied.

"Didn't realize you were coming," Lang remarked.

"I was in the area."

Neither of them acknowledged the fact that if that had been the case, he wouldn't have taken twenty minutes to arrive.

"You know *Dr.* Brown?" Lang asked, emphasizing Avery's title.

"I do. We grew up together."

"Ah." A shrewd light entered his eyes. "I see. Perhaps you can encourage her to be a little more forthcoming about the work she carries out here."

Gareth glanced at Avery and her chin jutted out defiantly. He was surprised to realize he didn't actually know what she did, beyond it being some kind of chemistry. Somehow, despite all the events they'd attended that had been hosted by mutual friends, she'd never shared details and he'd never asked.

"What are you working on, A-Bee?" he asked, the old nickname slipping out by mistake. When she scowled, he wished he could take it back. He'd undermined her authority in front of Lang.

"Like I told your buddy here, it's classified." Her eyebrows clashed over the bridge of her nose in a familiar stubborn expression. They weren't getting any information out of her. "If you want answers, ask your boss."

"Rata?" Lang asked, visibly startled. "You're doing work for us?"

Her expression didn't change. "As I said, I can't tell you."

A movement drew Gareth's gaze down and he noticed her hands were trembling. Likewise, her skin was pale and the freckles splashed across her nose stood out starkly. "You're going into shock," he told her. "Sit down. I'll get you a hot drink."

"You'll do no such thing, Gareth," she said. "I'm perfectly fine. If it weren't for this—"

The buzz of his personal radio interrupted her. He lifted it to his mouth. "Wayland here."

"Sergeant, I've had a report of a suspicious fire at 6 Ruataniwha Drive," the dispatcher said. "I repeat, a suspicious fire at 6 Ruataniwha Drive. The fire brigade are already on their way."

He didn't think it was possible, but Avery went even whiter.

"That's my house," she whispered.

Oh, *shit*. Gareth stared at the destruction around them and felt sick. This violence wasn't directed at the laboratory, it was targeted at Avery. Someone had it in for her.

"Copy," he said into the radio. "I'll be there soon."

ALSO BY ALEXA RIVERS

Little Sky Romance

Accidentally Yours

From Now Until Forever

It Was Always You

Dreaming of You

Little Sky Romance Novellas

Midnight Kisses

Second Chance Christmas

Haven Bay

Then There Was You

Two of a Kind

Safe in his Arms

If Only You Knew

Pretend to Be Yours

ACKNOWLEDGMENTS

To start with, thanks to my wonderful hubby who's been nothing but supportive during the years I've spent sitting in a corner, scribbling away. You answered the multitude of really random questions I ask which would probably concern someone else.

Thank you to my family for believing in me, encouraging my love of books, and reading some really terrible first drafts over the years with a smile and a kind word.

Thank you to my beta readers. To Carol D and Kate S, a big thank you for editing and proofreading Summer with the CEO and polishing it until it shone. Thank you to Deranged Doctor Design for my gorgeous cover.

Thank you to all of the members of Romance Writers of New Zealand who helped me iron out the kinks in my story, and to the 10 Minute Novelists Facebook group who encouraged me to get words on the page every day.

It's a pleasure to be part of the supportive writing community, which encourages people to believe in themselves.

ABOUT THE AUTHOR

Alexa Rivers writes about genuine characters living messy, imperfect lives and earning hard-won happily ever afters. Most of her books are set in small towns, and she lives in one of these herself. She shares a house with a neurotic dog and a husband who thinks he's hilarious.

When she's not writing, she enjoys traveling, baking, eating too much chocolate, cuddling fluffy animals, drinking excessive amounts of tea, and absorbing herself in fictional worlds.

Made in the USA
Monee, IL
12 May 2022